BLOODWOOD

Further Titles by Gillian Bradshaw from Severn House

THE ALCHEMY OF FIRE

DANGEROUS NOTES

THE WRONG REFLECTION

THE SOMERS TREATMENT

THE ELIXIR OF YOUTH

BLOODWOOD

BLOODWOOD

Gillian Bradshaw

This first world edition published in Great Britain 2007 by
SEVERN HOUSE PUBLISHERS LTD of
9–15 High Street, Sutton, Surrey SM1 1DF.
This first world edition published in the USA 2007 by
SEVERN HOUSE PUBLISHERS INC of
595 Madison Avenue, New York, N.Y. 10022.

British Library Cataloguing in Publication Data

Bradshaw, Gillian, 1956-
  Bloodwood
  1. Whistle blowing - Fiction
  2. Political ecology - Fiction
  3. Logging - Corrupt practices - Fiction
  4. Terminally ill - Fiction
  5. Suspense fiction
  I. Title
  813.5'4 [F]

  ISBN-13: 978-0-7278-6420-8

All Severn House titles are printed on acid-free paper.

Printed and bound in Great Britain by
MPG Books Ltd., Bodmin, Cornwall.

To Alan and to Mike and Helen
who are trying to save the planet

African Bloodwood
Pterocarpus angolensis
Southern Africa

Listed as 'vulnerable' on the World Conservation
Union's Red list

One

I didn't think much of Dr Hillman. It was true I'd only met the man twice before, but with doctors that's usually enough. The test is whether they'll talk to you: most of them merely tick questions off some diagnostic check-list. The diagnosis itself, in these cases, has always been made before-hand, from some cursory glance over your notes. If a doctor talks to you, it means he's willing to listen to the symptoms as described by an ignorant patient: he hasn't automatically assumed that you're a whinging hypochondriac and completely unreliable. He'll see you as a person; he has an open mind.

Dr Hillman hadn't talked to me. A plump, self-satisfied prig of a consultant, in our first meeting he hadn't even made eye contact: his attention had been on his notes and his computer. He had ticked off the boxes on his mental check-list, then sent me off for tests with a dismissive smirk and a scrawled signature on a form. At the second meeting he'd frowned and ordered more tests without explaining the results of any of the first ones.

In retrospect, I should have realized it was a bad sign that he met my eyes when I entered his office for the third time.

'Ms Lanchester,' he said, and got up to shake hands. 'Please, sit down.'

I sat in the chair he indicated – a cheap office job, metal frame with a seat padded in charcoal, thirty pounds or so from MFI. I arranged my hands on top of my Dolce & Gabbana handbag and gave the doctor a sharp look. I'd woken up with the headache again, and I had an important meeting scheduled at the office later that day: I didn't feel particu-larly inclined to either patience or good nature.

'Ms Lanchester,' he said again, and then seemed at a loss.

I nodded at the cardboard folder on his desk to make him get to the point. 'Are those the results of my tests?'

He picked the folder up. 'Yes.' He met my eyes for the second time since I came in. 'Ms Lanchester, I'm afraid I have some bad news for you.'

Oh, God. Surgery. I hate hospitals. I didn't know how I'd get the time off work. The office had been very busy recently.

Dr Hillman riffled through the folder as though relieved to have something to occupy his hands. 'Your, uh, headaches,' he began. 'They're being caused by pressure inside the skull. This result here, see?' He extended a sheet to me. 'The ophthalmoscope test. It shows a distinct papilloedema – that is, a bulge in the optic disk at the back of your eye. A swelling of the optic disk is normally a sign of raised intracranial pressure.'

That fitted well with the incidents of blurred and doubled vision I'd been suffering. I nodded impatiently.

He looked up and met my eyes yet again. 'Pressure inside the skull, that means.'

'Yes, doctor,' I said irritably. 'I understood it the first time you said it. So: I have raised intracranial pressure, and it's pushing against the back of my eyes and giving me blurred vision and headaches. What can you do about it?'

'Ah. Well. I can give you a prescription for a drug called dexamethasone. It should reduce the pressure on your brain and give you some relief from the symptoms.'

'From the *symptoms*,' I repeated sharply. 'Doctor, I'm happy if you can relieve the symptoms – but what about the *cause*?'

The smug consultant actually bit his lip. He pulled a CD out of the folder and inserted it into his computer. A 3-D image appeared in false colour: my MRI scan. The doctor rotated that morbid vision of the skull beneath the skin, then shifted the cursor. 'Here,' he said, pointing with the image in three-quarter profile. 'You see this?'

He was indicating a spot behind my right ear. What was I supposed to say? 'Nice resolution on the temporal bones'? 'No,' I replied firmly instead.

'Here,' said Dr Hillman, and pointed again.

Shock isn't really a sensation of *cold*, although it's often described that way. It's more as though a part of the world has been stripped away from your cosy, squirming, vulnerable self, leaving you exposed, like a blind kitten in its nest. There was, yes, a shadow on the image – a faint smudge, a smoke-shrimp, curled with its little claws digging in behind my ear and its fat tail trailing off toward the back of my skull.

'It's a tumour,' said the doctor, ruthless now that he'd brought himself to the point. 'Almost certainly a high-grade astrocytoma. Given the developmental pattern, that is, and the results of some of your other tests.'

I wanted to shriek, 'You're saying I have *brain cancer*?' but somehow I couldn't. It was as though naming it would give it power. I sat there, clutching my expensive handbag and staring.

Dr Hillman burbled on, explaining that astrocytomas were the commonest form of . . . yes, *brain cancer*. He explained that they were gliomas – that is, cancers of the glial cells, which are support systems for the neurons. Astrocytes, he informed me, are a form of glial cell, named for their vaguely star-shaped appearance.

Astronomy, I thought. Astrology; astroturf. Astrocytoma: a star gone bad inside my head, a private black hole. *Brain cancer*, oh my God!

'What . . .' I began. The doctor instantly stopped burbling. I licked my lips. 'How . . . What do you have to do to get rid of it?'

Silence. I should have comprehended that silence, but I didn't. I was still thinking *brain cancer, oh, God, how much damage is it doing? How much damage will it do when they dig it out? Am I going to stay normal? Will I lose my job?* and even, with stupid vanity, *Am I going to lose all my hair?*

Dr Hillman rotated the CT image. 'Look.' He indicated another spot, which, to my ignorant eyes, looked just like every other spot on the scan.

'Look at *what*?' I snarled resentfully.

'Here.' He tapped it. 'This blood vessel.'

'Oh.' I could see it, after all: the graphic had coloured it red.

'It's already been constricted by the growth of the tumour.

That, *there*, further in – that's the brain stem. The pressure . . . you see where that artery comes from, how it goes right there? We can't operate on this tumour, Ms Lanchester.'

'But, but . . .' I stared at him in bewilderment. 'I thought these days you could operate on *anything*! What about laser surgery? Or, or microwaves? Or . . .'

'We *can't* operate, Ms Lanchester. There is no way we can cut that tumour out without killing you. I'm very sorry. Now, we will need to do a biopsy, to confirm the diagnosis, but I'm already ninety-nine percent sure there is nothing we can do. Given how quickly this cancer appeared and how much it's grown just since your first scan, I'd say it's particularly aggressive. If it's a glioma – and I'm sure it is – it will already have infiltrated all the surrounding tissue. Radio- and chemotherapy will be no use. There is no treatment that would give you any clinical benefit. I'm sorry.'

I stared at him, speechless. It isn't quite true to say that I couldn't take it in. I understood what he was saying: I simply couldn't believe it. I was thirty-nine. I had woken up, yes, with a headache, but also with worries from the office and a resolve to look into a holiday in the Caribbean over Christmas. How could everything in my life suddenly become *irrelevant*?

Hillman swallowed. 'We can do several things to make you more comfortable. The dexamethasone will relieve the intracranial pressure, and we can give you some anti-inflammatories as well. We can discuss other forms of pain relief and anti-convulsants when that, um, becomes relevant.'

I glared at him, suddenly furious – with his plump, self-satisfied face, his incomprehensible scan, his shallow sympathy. Probably he'd had a lecture on how to break the bad news to a patient: tell them you're very sorry, and make sure you discuss pain relief. He was talking about *letting me die*!

'I want a second opinion!' I cried.

He only nodded, with a knowing air, as though this was a standard reaction. 'Of course. I can arrange it, if you like. Or, if you prefer, you can choose another consultant and I'll arrange for him to see your scans.' He hesitated, then went on, 'Um. We're probably dealing with a very aggressive cancer. You will, um, need to make it clear that you need an opinion *urgently*.'

Another layer of reality seemed to slide away. I felt like a rabbit, being forced from one dug-up tunnel after another, out towards the exit where the dogs were waiting. 'How urgently?'

'I'm sorry . . .'

'No you're *not!*' I shouted it, the shrill hysterical sound of my voice shocking me. I paused, swallowed, then went on, just as vehemently but more quietly. 'You're just uncomfortable and embarrassed and looking forward to getting this out of the way: you don't really give a damn about *me*! How long do I have?'

He blinked. He didn't get angry, though: the expression on his face was, unmistakably, pity. He drew a deep breath. 'At worst, two months. It could be more, of course, but not more than six. And . . . I *am* very sorry.'

I sat, staring at him. Cold? Yes. Cold as the grave, wherein my love is lain.

Dr Hillman began speaking again, telling me about the tumour and what I could expect of it, advising me what I should and should not do. I stared at his lips moving, but his words made no sense. After a time he seemed to realize that, and he handed me a print-out. 'This contains the information I've just given you,' he said. He added a prescription and a pink hospital slip. 'That's for the dexamethasone. That's for your next appointment. You should come back in a couple of days. I'll discuss the prognosis with you, and we can arrange a time for the biopsy.'

'A biopsy,' I said, clutching at straws. 'If you still need to do that, doesn't it mean . . .'

He shook his head without waiting for me to finish. 'If the biopsy shows that this is a low-grade cancer and that we can treat it, I'll be absolutely delighted – but I'm sorry, I don't expect it, and it would be wrong to get your hopes up. Did you come with someone today?'

'No.'

'Then maybe you should phone a friend to take you home. Whatever you do, don't drive.' He smiled appeasingly. 'You need to stop driving at once: that's a legal requirement. If you need some help getting home, the receptionist can arrange it.'

I let him escort me to the office door, then walked out of Neurology without stopping. Only when I reached my car did I realize I was still clutching the pink slip.

I did not go back in to make my next appointment. Instead I unlocked the car, slid into the driving seat, and stared out the windscreen at the hospital car park. It was a grey day in late October, and everything was wet and littered with sodden dead leaves. The car park was overcrowded, every slot taken and cars parked on the grass verge. A red Nissan cruised down the lane behind me, saw me sitting in my Porsche, and stopped hopefully.

I turned the key in the ignition and backed out, very carefully. The Nissan pulled gratefully into my space. Others would take my place in life just as eagerly, when I was cold and dead.

Cold and dead. 'When I am cold and dead and laid in grave . . .' Where was that from? I couldn't place it. I drove out of the hospital, navigated the roundabout, and started home, driving with great care, seeing nothing. In two to six months, the black hole inside my skull would have sucked me in, and I would be forever beyond its event horizon – lost in the country 'from whose bourn no traveller returns'. To be, or, in my case, not to be. Never again to fall in love, laugh at a joke, savour a nice shiraz. Never, never, never. Cold and dead. Cold and dead.

I arrived back at my apartment and parked the car neatly in my numbered slot. The garage was almost empty: it was half past twelve, lunchtime, and people were at work. I took the lift up the dozen floors to my flat.

I'd bought the place three years before, after the divorce. It was officially part of a 'luxury redevelopment'called Canalside. My flat wasn't quite a penthouse, though it was near the top of the fifteen-storey building, and had a view out over the eponymous canal. It hadn't been new when I bought it, but it had been in immaculate condition. I'd had it redecorated anyway, and bought some furniture at the company's hefty discount. It was a beautiful place now, all cream carpets and gleaming tropical hardwoods. When I came in it had a superficial untidiness, with a couple of days' worth of newspapers sitting on the coffee table, together with two coffee mugs and a Royal Derby plate holding a torn orange peel. Beneath those small blemishes, though, everything was clean, elegant, civilized: the cleaning lady had come on Monday. The two large bookcases held rows of neatly shelved titles; the racks either side of the music centre held CDs arranged by composer; on the wall was a framed print of Renoir's 'The Boating Party Lunch'. Universal entropy, proclaimed the room, is held at bay. Beyond the picture window, the canal lay dark and sullen under the heavy skies.

I set the pink appointment slip down on the kitchen counter and put the electric kettle on. Then I switched it off again, and got myself a stiff drink.

Cold and dead. I might insist on a second opinion, but I knew it would do me no good. Nothing would do me any good: not healthy exercise, not red wine or green tea; not sleep therapy or carrot juice; not vitamin pills or high-protein diets. There was no *good* any more – only two to six months, and then the long step into the everlasting.

I finished the drink, got myself another. An automatic censor warned me that the alcohol would make my headache worse – and then I remembered that it *didn't matter*, because there was nothing that could make my headache better.

Halfway through the second drink I remember the meeting that had seemed important that morning: a couple of trade journalists willing to do a review of our new line of kitchens. *Fuck kitchens*, I told myself, but the image of my bewildered assistant persecuted me. I imagined Kath's breathless voice over the phone. *'Toni? Where are you? Those guys from* Furniture Today *are here now!'*

I phoned the office. 'Masterpiece Home Design, Public Relations,' said Kath cheerfully. 'May I help you?'

'It's me,' I told her. 'Kath, I'm sorry, but you need to cancel that meeting this afternoon.'

'You OK?' she asked, the concern in her voice telling me that I didn't sound it.

'Yeah, I'm fine. I just . . . had to have another test, and they put some stuff in my eyes. They're streaming, and my nose has decided to keep them company. I'm not fit to be seen in public. Please give *Furniture Today* my sincere apologies.'

'Oh, you poor thing!' exclaimed Kath sympathetically. 'Don't they know what's wrong yet?'

'Pressure at the back of my eyes, they said, but they don't know why. Look, if there isn't time to cancel *Furniture Today*, give them the stuff we printed up, and you and Tom show them the display. I have to take the rest of today off, but I'll be in tomorrow.'

'OK.' She was completely reassured. 'Hope you feel better soon!'

Vain hope. I switched off the phone and picked up my drink again, wondering why I had lied.

How could I have told the truth? 'Please cancel the meeting this afternoon: I've just been told I have less than six months to live.' It was too huge a thing. I needed to get my own mind around it before I could tell anyone else. Then, too, the urge to *protect my job* seemed to have become a spinal reflex, independent of the brain. *Don't tell the company anything that might make them get rid of you.* Masterpiece Home Design did not go in for benevolent paternalism. Fall ill or pregnant, take time off to care for your sick mother or disabled child, and you'd soon find yourself unemployed. They were careful about it, of course – there was never anything anyone could take to an employment tribunal – but everybody in the company knew the score.

I made up my mind to quit, as soon as I had my second opinion – or maybe even before. It looked like I wasn't going to need a job any more, and if it came right down to it, I didn't much *like* Masterpiece Home Design, and hadn't from the first moment I started working for them. They'd head-hunted me for the PR job, which had been flattering, and they'd offered a lot of money at a time when I needed it, but I'd had misgivings about them from the first brief they gave me.

People often describe public relations as a form of glori-fied lying, but it's never felt like that to me. It ought to be about *communication*, about finding some point where a client's concerns intersect with the world of the woman in the street, so that what had been boring or esoteric suddenly becomes vivid and alive for her. At the firm where I started out, one of our clients was a pet food company. When I talked to them, I found that they produced a low-sodium line for dogs with kidney problems. A few phone calls found me an old lady whose ancient and much-loved spaniel relied on it, and *bingo*, I had a human-interest story the media couldn't resist, and the pet food producers had a caring image. Oh, sure, there's another side to pet food too: an abattoir full of slaughtered animal carcasses, stinking offal and the danger of bacterial contamination. The old lady and her spaniel, though, are just as real and true. PR doesn't actually *deny* the existence of the abattoir; it just draws attention to the spaniel.

There was an abattoir behind Masterpiece Home Design, too, and they'd had me denying it from the moment I was hired.

I leaned forward and ran my hand over the polished surface of the occasional table beside my chair. It was a beautiful rich red-brown: the heartwood of the African tree called wild teak, or mukwa, or kiaat, or bloodwood. They say the sap is the exact colour of blood, and that people in the countries where it grows use it as a dye.

Bloodwood isn't officially endangered, although it is being overlogged, can't be grown in plantations and in most parts of its range the trees are dying off because of a fungus. Still, it's a valuable source of foreign currency for a number of countries that don't have many others. By the standards of Masterpiece Home Design, it was an ethically responsible choice for furniture. There were other woods used in MHD products that had less savoury origins.

I'd frequently told the media that all the timber used in Masterpiece products was legally sold, which was true. Timber cut against the law in its country of origin can still be legally sold when it gets to Britain. If an Indonesian or Brazilian company bulldozes its way into a bit of protected rainforest, takes a chainsaw to the trees, and silences the officials of its own government with threats or bribes, that's a matter for the local government. It's not the business of a Western furniture retailer – not even if the retailer knows damn well what's going on, and makes it worth the loggers' while.

I'd got used to flicking over the television to a different channel whenever a wildlife documentary came on with its inevitable pleas to *save the rainforests*; I'd been managing to ignore the queasy feeling in my stomach when I read about global warming and the evil consequences of deforestation. After all, it really *isn't* the job of a Western company to enforce laws in the developing world. The people who scream about irresponsible multinationals are, by and large, the same ones who scream about *interfering* multinationals that think they know better than elected governments. Increasingly, though, I'd begun to suspect that my employers had done worse than merely buy illegally sourced timber. I'd never tried to confirm what I suspected. I'd preferred not to know.

Now I wondered why. I'd stuck with this damned job for three years. Why hadn't I handed in my resignation and done something *useful* instead – something I could look back on with *pride*?

The money, of course. MHD paid well. People looked at me and saw a 'successful career woman' with a beautiful flat, expensive clothing, and two foreign holidays a year. They didn't see a failed poet with a broken marriage and a job she despised. It had mattered to me that they shouldn't.

Now my successful career was almost at an end, and what good had it done me? I would leave behind the flat, the clothes, the glories of the world I'd seen and those I hadn't – and as soon as I was gone, it would be as though I'd never lived. I wished I'd had children, or written a book, or supported orphans in Africa or something – anything – so that there was one thing I could point to and say, 'Look! I made a difference!' Instead, I would leave only silence. I would probably die sometime during the bleak, dull, dirty-gray days of January or February, out of my mind on morphine in the overcrowded squalor of a hospital ward.

I would have to make sure I hired a firm to clean out my flat before then, as my mother would find that an intolerable burden. As it was she'd be devastated – *and* she'd feel I'd let her down by dying before she did. My brother would be unhappy – and irritated, because he'd then be obliged to do more for my mother. My ex, Ian, would probably shed a few tears – and *definitely* try to claim a share in the estate, such as it was.

I could feel the headache beginning again, pressing against the back of my eyes. I finished my drink and went to the bathroom for a couple of co-codamols, although you're not supposed to mix them with alcohol. Popping the pills into my hand, I suddenly considered finishing the packet, and then finishing the bottle of Scotch. The end was too horrible to contemplate, so why not get it over with immediately?

Probably, though, it wouldn't work. There was only about a third of a bottle of Scotch left, and about half a dozen pills. I would just wake up next morning, sick and groggy and smelling of vomit. If I wanted to kill myself I'd have to go down to the shops and buy more booze and more pain-killers. It was just too hard to do in cold blood. Besides, I had two to six months left to live – why cheat myself even of that?

Oh, that classic question: 'If you knew you had only a few months to live, what would you do?' I might as well come up with an answer to it.

I swallowed the co-codamol with a glass of water, then went back into the kitchen and put on the kettle.

So what *would* I do with my few remaining weeks? A grand tour of the world? How much did a round-the-world cruise cost?

I went to my computer, switched it on, and Googled 'round-the-world cruise'. Lots of hits: the cost seemed to be between six and twelve thousand pounds, depending on the cruise company and the class of accommodation. I checked my bank account.

The current account was healthy, as it usually was at the end of the month – my paycheck went in on or around the 21st. There wasn't much in savings, though – only about two thousand pounds, the minimal buffer I'd allowed myself for repairs to the flat or the car. The credit card account, which had a limit of five thousand, was in a better state: it had only a couple of hundred on it. I could, if I liked, book myself one of the cheaper world cruises on the spot.

I could undoubtedly borrow enough money for a luxury

cruise, too. I could sell the car – *ought* to sell the car, if I was officially forbidden to drive it. There was my pension fund as well – God, I'd paid into that all my working life, what a waste! Pensions weren't straightforward, but presumably I could get out *something* of what I'd put in. I could splash out on a private cabin on the QE2, if I wanted to!

Except that it suddenly seemed *pointless*. I didn't really want to spend my last weeks of life gliding from place to place in sanitized comfort on some moving city full of shops and discos and swimming pools, surrounded by elderly Americans. I wanted the *world*, in all its wonder and horror, and I wanted it for my full three-score-years-and-ten.

I slammed my fist down on the mouse-mat, then sat, breathing hard, waiting for the tears.

They would not come. Maybe I didn't yet believe in my own death; maybe I was just too angry to cry. My eyes stayed dry, though my vision began to blur and the headache got worse.

I got up and made myself a cup of tea, then sat down on the sofa. Cradling the mug in my lap, I leaned my head back and stared up at the ceiling.

After a while I found myself watching the shadows up there. They were long leaf shadows cast, I supposed, by sunlight reflected off the canal. They shifted as the wind moved, dappling the white plaster with a restful pattern of light and dark. I stared at them for several minutes before I remembered that the trees by the canal were bare, and that the day had been sullen and overcast. I sat up.

A diffuse green light was streaming through the window, and I could see branches moving beyond it. I knew it was impossible: I was a dozen storeys up, and the tallest of the trees along the canal barely topped eight metres. I stared in bewilderment, then turned to set my tea down on the occasional table.

The table was bleeding. I recoiled in horror, spilling tea, and gazed at it, stricken. Thick red gore oozed from the wood and trickled down the legs to the cream-coloured carpet. I looked round, horrified, and saw that the arms of the easy chairs, the television stand, the desk, were all bleeding like freshly slaughtered meat. The light from the window swayed over the scene, dappling it with green shade.

I got to my feet, still clutching the tea. My head was pounding and I felt sick. I walked over to the window and looked out.

It was green, green everywhere. The branches of the great trees swayed in the wind, lianas dripping from their limbs; butterflies drifted, and here and there the wings of some tropical bird flashed brilliance. There was no sound, though: no rustling of the leaves, no calling of the birds, only a profound stillness.

I closed my eyes. Lights pulsed red behind the lids. Suddenly I felt horribly sick. I turned away from the window, staggered to the bathroom, and vomited up what was left of two Scotch-and-sodas, two co-codamols, and half a cup of tea. Then I collapsed on to the bath mat, pressing my hands against my throbbing eyes.

After a while, the pain receded a bit. I fumbled the towel off the rack to wrap around me, because I was cold. A little later I felt well enough to stand up.

I washed my face in the sink and looked up groggily at my reflection: a pale, haggard face stared back at me, brown hair dishevelled, eyes blackly dilated. I wrung out the washcloth and put it across my forehead, then, still hugging the towel around my shoulders, went cautiously back into the sitting room.

Everything was exactly as it should be: cream carpet, hardwood furniture upholstered in ochre and gold, two empty coffee cups, one tea cup – on its side by the window – and a plate with an orange peel. No leaf shadows, no blood. I went to the window and looked out: there below was the canal, sullen and dark under the grey October sky, flanked by black, denuded sycamores. I looked incredulously at the spot where the occasional table had been oozing on to the carpet. There was a splash there, but when I went over to check, it turned out to be tea.

Numbly, I sat on the sofa again. After a minute or two, I remembered the print-out Dr Hillman had given me, and got up to search for it.

I'd left it in the kitchen with the pink appointment slip. I took it back to the sitting room and switched on the lights: the grey daylight was beginning to fade.

I found what I was looking for on the second page. 'Patients with tumours that affect the visual cortex (at the back of the head) may find they suffer visual deficits or hallucinations.' The tail of that smoke-shrimp had indeed trailed round to the back of my head, so I supposed I had a 'tumour affecting the visual cortex'.

Shit. So that had been a hallucination? It had seemed as real as the view out the window, as real as everything else I'd seen that day.

I sat huddled on the sofa while outside the dusk faded into dark. The headache receded slowly, leaving weariness in its place. The hallucination had left me shaken, and as I thought about it, I realized that what had shaken me most was the form it took.

Oh, I could explain it. I'd inadvisedly had two drinks and downed two co-codamols, so my over-pressured, inflamed brain had flipped on me. There was no mystery to it. The trouble was, there was also no mystery to why I'd seen my furniture – my MHD staff-discount furniture – bleeding. MHD had sinned, and I had told lies to defend them. The blood I'd seen on my furniture was metaphorically on my hands.

Eventually I got up, went to the kitchen, and warmed up a tin of lentil soup. I sat down at the breakfast bar to eat it, and tried not to look at the smooth teak surface my bowl sat upon. I had only a few months to live. What should I do with my final weeks?

I'd told Kath I'd go in to work tomorrow. I could find out whether what I suspected was true – and, if it was, I could blow the whistle. *That* would make a difference; *that* would be something on which I could look back with pride.

For the first time since I'd heard the news, I found it in myself to smile.

Satinwood
Chloroxylon Swietenia
Southern India and Sri Lanka

Listed as 'Vulnerable' on the Red list

Two

I drove in to work. I suppose it was an irresponsible thing to do, but it had been perfectly legal the morning before, and I couldn't really believe that I'd degenerated *that* much in just twenty-four hours. Besides, people at work would have found it odd if I'd taken a taxi.

The headquarters of Masterpiece Home Design was part of a business park. That conjures up a string of pre-fabs flanked by parking, let out to e-businesses and printers, which is altogether the wrong image. No, think of the sort of business park that is situated in landscaped grounds on the outskirts of a town, with a drive planted with young flowering cherries in cardboard tubes – a drive which sweeps about a lake where a fountain plays, and debouches into a series of discreet car parks enclosed by beds of ornamental shrubs, beyond which rise tall glass-fronted edifices.

The management considered this to be plebeian. The glossy brochures and promotional videos I helped to produce tended to be shot in elegant eighteenth-century stately homes, and contained endless pictures of MHD's smiling, white-haired director walking through high-ceilinged, chandeliered rooms, gesturing at his beautiful furniture. He was known to have wanted to buy an eighteenth-century house in London as the company headquarters. They couldn't really justify the expense, though, and at MHD all expenses had to be justified. The company's products were aimed squarely at a growing market: a middle class willing to splash out on an occasional luxury item. That meant keeping the overheads down. People who are used to spending three hundred pounds on a sofa may be willing to pay three thousand, if they think they're getting something to boast about; ask for four thousand, however, and they'll end up back at Ikea.

I parked and made my way over to the entrance. The gold-tinted glass provided a view of the potted plants and small fountain in the foyer, and also of the receptionist at her desk. I ran my key-card through the slot, nodded to the receptionist, and took the lift to my office on the first floor.

As usual, I was the first in Public Relations to arrive. I unlocked the doors, went through to my own office, and turned on the computer.

There was a flagged email from my boss. *See me when you get in.* That would be about missing the *Furniture Today* feature. I defiantly checked the rest of the inbox first, deleted half of it and started to answer the rest.

Kath came in while I was engaged in this. She was a small, vivacious woman, a few years younger than me, who always wore the most marvellously coordinated outfits. Today she had on a gold lamé top, gold shoes, a gold belt, with gold hair clips in her curly black hair. I would miss Kath. She smiled warmly when she saw me, and asked how I was feeling.

'Not too bad,' I lied, and chatted for a minute about *Furniture Today*. 'I have an email from Ken,' I told her. 'Bet you it's a ticking-off about letting the media down.'

'It wasn't *your* fault!' exclaimed Kath indignantly.

'You think that makes a difference? Don't worry; I have no intention of letting him blame me.' I picked up my handbag and went to face the music.

Kenneth Norman, my boss, was the member of MHD's board charged with overseeing advertising as well as public relations. He was a short, stout, bad-tempered man – a bully, but a cowardly one, who backed down quickly if you stood up to him. His suits were always a size too small around the waist: optimism, I suppose. In the mornings his stomach bulged over the top of his trousers; by evening he would have undone a button and loosened his belt, and one had glimpses of his briefs. His office was on the third floor – an immense room, where his eighteenth-century-inspired desk with its satinwood veneer loomed like a reef amid a sea of Axminster carpet. When I came in he glowered and looked pointedly at his watch.

'I'm sorry I didn't come at once,' I said, smiling at him,

taking a seat on the flimsy-looking chair, crossing an immaculately waxed and nyloned leg. I'd put on my grey silk business suit that morning, picking the colour to make myself appear less washed-out, and I knew it looked sharp enough to cut bone. *Terminal cancer, me?* 'I had some emails which required urgent attention.' *No, I didn't get in late*, that meant, and *I'm conscientious and hard-working.* 'What was it you wanted to see me about, Ken?' We were all on first-name terms at MHD, a superficial chumminess that fooled no one.

Ken glowered harder and arranged his pudgy hands on the golden wood. 'Yesterday you missed an important meeting with representatives of the media!' he told me reprovingly.

'Yes,' I agreed. 'I was so annoyed about that! It took me weeks to set it up.' *They wouldn't have been here at all*, that reminded him, *if I hadn't arranged it.*

'It's very regrettable!' he huffed.

'Yes,' I agreed again. There was a silence, and then I asked politely, 'What was it you wanted to see me about?'

That wrong-footed him. 'A public relations officer should not, uh, cancel meetings with important media outlets at such short notice!'

'Ken, it's not as though I had a *choice* about it! I had a reaction to some eye-drops the hospital used in a test. I had to spend the afternoon lying down with a cold cloth over my eyes. It was no fun at all, and it was very frustrating. I worked hard to set up that meeting. For Christ's sake, if I'd been rammed by some joyrider on the way back from the hospital, would you hold me responsible for *that*?'

'What a–a *spurious* comparison! *You* chose to schedule that test in work time!'

'For goodness' sake! When *else* do hospitals schedule appointments? Look, I've had exactly three medical appointments in the past quarter. Are you telling me that this places an intolerable burden on the company and amounts to a failure to do my job properly?'

He opened his mouth, closed it, then snapped, 'Of course not! All I'm saying is that it was *regrettable* that this interfered with your work, and that you need to do your best to ensure that it doesn't happen again.'

'I see. And how do you suggest I sort out my health problem

without making any medical appointments? I missed – what was it? – *nine* hours of work this quarter for medical appointments, plus two days for the flu. How does that compare with the average employee?'

He leaned back in his place, face flushed.

'Shall we look at personnel records?' I suggested. I got to my feet, went around his desk, and looked down at the computer. It was switched on, and had a screensaver of mountains. Ken flinched away as I leaned over him. I jiggled the mouse, and it immediately came up with a request for the password.

'All I meant to say,' snapped Ken, gathering up the scraps of his dignity, 'was that it was regrettable that you cancelled your meeting with *Furniture Today* at such short notice.'

I smiled sweetly at him, still leaning over him. That wasn't all he'd meant to say, of course. He'd meant to foster the company ethos: that MHD owned every hour of its employees' days, that illness or family commitments amounted to theft of company property. He'd wanted to force me on the defensive for taking sick leave when I went to see a doctor; he expected me to be grateful when he decided to overlook the failing.

'Shall we just look at personnel?' I coaxed. 'See how my two days plus nine hours compares to the average?' *Come on, Ken! Type in your password!*

He glared.

'It's much better than the average, isn't it?' I taunted him. 'Other people take *twice* as much, is my bet.'

'Not that good,' he snarled, and typed in the password.

He was, as I knew very well, a two-finger hunt-and-peck typist, and catching the word was no trouble: SLALOM. Who'd have thought he'd go for something so sporty?

The average sick leave for MHD employees per quarter turned out to be four days. 'See?' Ken pointed out triumphantly. 'It's nowhere near twice as much!'

I smiled. 'It's more than *I* took, though, Ken.'

He grunted. 'The point *is*,' he said testily, 'you missed an important meeting!'

'Very much against my wishes,' I pointed out. 'And not because of anything I could have foreseen. Are you going to sack me for it?'

'Of course not! I just . . . I just didn't appreciate that you had a *reaction* to this test. I thought it was something *foreseeable.*'

'Was there anything else you wanted to talk to me about? Then I should be getting back to my work. Thank you, Ken, for asking: they haven't yet found out what's wrong, but I'm feeling quite a lot better today.'

I left, knowing I'd annoyed him, and that now he *would* sack me, if I gave him the slightest excuse. It gave me a wonderful sense of power to be in position where I couldn't care less.

I spent the rest of the day dealing with the post and trying to get my department's affairs in order. I might despise my employers, but that was no reason to add to the burdens of my unfortunate successor by leaving the office in a mess. It didn't actually need too much effort on my part: I'd always been well organized.

Kath went home at five. When she said goodbye I told her I'd just finish what was I doing, and then lock up. I finished sorting out a file, then sat at my desk, listening as the sounds of the building gradually faded from voices and closing doors to the background creaks and humming. From my window I had a view over the car park. It was already too dark to see much, but the steady succession of red tail lights leaving the car park was clear enough. The executives' cars were parked in reserved slots next to the entrance, where the gold-tinted light from the foyer illumined them: Mercedes, BMW, Land Rover. MHD managers had a long-hours culture: it was nearly six before the first of those reserved slots emptied. Ken's silver-grey Mercedes pulled out at quarter past six.

I armed myself with a set of print-outs I'd selected during the course of the day, got a key from the security guard's office on the grounds that I needed to drop them off, and went upstairs to Ken's office. I dropped the print-outs in his assistant's in-tray, then continued into his palatial office. I did not turn on the light; someone might notice it shining through the window. Instead I seated myself at the satin-wood desk and switched on the computer. It asked for the password, and I typed in SLALOM.

Going through someone else's computer is probably more
intimate than searching their bedroom. I'd half expected the
files of porn, and they didn't seem to be anything particularly objectionable, just pouting sluts with improbable breasts
– no little girls, no violence. What was I to make, though,
of the photos of mountains? There were megabytes of them:
rock and snow, ice, crevasses, glaciers, and bare peaks biting
savagely at cobalt skies. Occasionally there would be an
anoraked figure in a corner somewhere, but in most of the
pictures there was no human presence, and there was never
anything to identify the location. I was fairly sure that Ken
didn't climb mountains. What did it mean to him, when he
looked at these pictures?

None of my business. I couldn't find what I was looking
for in the document files or the desktop, and eventually
resorted to the 'Find File' function, typing in keywords.
Sarawak, Penan . . .

I eventually found it under 'Magoh River', an unlisted file.
I printed it, found another file linked to it, and printed that.

I stopped for a moment then, hands on the keyboard. If I
took my two documents to the public, MHD would just
dismiss them as forgeries – but I was afraid to go on. It's
hard to say quite why: if Ken himself had come in just then,
he wouldn't have done anything worse than shout at me to
get out and tell me that I'd be sacked for misconduct. It was
nearly eight by then, though, and the building was dark and
still. Outside the window, the car park was empty in the
orange neon. My head was throbbing, and my heart was full
of dread. There was blood in those unlisted files, large quan-
tities of it.

I'd found another keyword, though, in the 'Magoh River'
file: Sulong Logging. I typed it in, and found a file. When
I opened it, I saw that it was a financial spreadsheet, with
dates and amounts and account numbers: a smoking gun.

I was surprised: Ken had nothing to do with accounting.
Presumably he'd been given the other files so that he'd know
what to steer people away from, but there seemed no reason
for him to have the incriminating details of the finance.
Perhaps he'd wondered, some cold night, just how deep the
dirt went, and dug into the company's accounts to see for

himself – and then, when he had his answer, buried it away and tried not to think about it. At any rate, he'd left me some evidence that could not be dismissed.

I printed out the 'Sulong Logging' file, then shut down the computer and sat for a moment in the empty office. The only light was the car park neon, which cast the shadows of lamps and monitors against the far wall, large and monstrous, like prehistoric reptiles. I closed my eyes, afraid of what my brain might see, and listened to my own strained breathing. The heating system clunked.

After a few long, undisturbed minutes, I opened my eyes, shuffled the print-outs together, and remembered to switch off the printer. I locked the office, returned the key to the guard's office, and went home.

The next day was a Friday, and I phoned in sick. I suppose I should have pretended that all was normal and gone in to work, but now that I had my print-outs safely home I felt as though I'd stolen treasure from a dragon's lair while the great beast slept, and that if I returned while it was awake I would be consumed. I told Kath that the headache was very bad and that I hoped to get the results of my tests that morning, accepted her sympathy, and cut off.

After that I was a good girl, and attended to setting my affairs in order. I phoned Neurology, and fixed a time for my follow-up appointment with Dr Hillman. I phoned my pension fund manager, inquired about cashing in, and was promised that I would be sent a form. Then I walked down to the local shops to pick up some groceries and my prescription.

It was another chill, dank October morning. It had rained again during the night, and the streets were wet. I walked briskly, thumb looped through the strap of my handbag. It had been months since I'd walked to the shops, rather than driving, and years since I'd been on a work day. Everything seemed very quiet. I saw no one on the way there, and when I reached the little parade the people were different from the ones I encountered at weekends: elderly, or young mothers with pushchairs. There were no women my age, and no men of working age at all.

I collected my prescription and some more co-codamol,

purchased bread, fresh fruit and some ready meals, and started home.

The sun came out when I was about a block from home. The street was lined with beeches, which still had their gold-russet leaves, and suddenly the branches above my head seemed illumined from within. The wet tarmac glowed golden, and the windows of all the buildings along the street blazed in the light. Even the damp air seemed to shine, as though the sun had dissolved in it, so that I was breathing light. I stopped where I stood, paralysed by the beauty of it, the inexplicable glory of the world, opening like a revelation to me, who was soon to leave it.

That was when the tears came: in the street, a block from home, while I had a bag of groceries in each hand. They came in floods, irresistible. I wanted to sit down on the curb and give way to them, but it was too wet to sit. I struggled on home, mouth open, nose running, eyes streaming, made it up to the flat, and collapsed by the window, looking at the sunlight on the canal and weeping uncontrollably, because that light would soon be gone.

That afternoon I drafted my resignation notice and phoned the office.

'Masterpiece Home Design, Public Relations!' said Kath brightly.

'It's me.'

There was a silence. I realized that so far, I'd told no one. Kath would be the first and easiest: after her I would have to inform . . .

I didn't want to inform my mother or my brother; I would put that off.

'Are you all right?' asked Kath, very concerned.

'No,' I confessed. 'Kath, I'm sorry to throw this at you, but I'm handing in my notice. I've been told I have terminal brain cancer. Please could—'

She didn't let me finish. She began a series of horrified exclamations: 'Oh, Toni! Oh, God! Oh, how terrible!' then tried to tell me that the hospital must have got it wrong. Every word she said made me feel worse, and I couldn't bear it. After a couple of minutes, I hung up.

I found an envelope for my resignation letter, stuck a first-class stamp on it, and put it in the post. While I was returning to the flat, my mobile rang. It was Ken.

'What the fuck are you playing at?' he demanded angrily.

This was outrageous, even for Ken. 'I don't have to take this!' I told him angrily.

'You do if you want to stay with this company!'

'Ha! I just posted my resignation.'

'Your what?'

'My resignation, Ken. My notice. I've had enough of MHD.'

A brief, astonished silence. 'You . . . you can't *resign* just like that! You need . . .'

'Technically, yes, I need to give a month's notice, but I'm resigning on health grounds, with immediate effect. Come off it: you know the company isn't suddenly going to come over all compassionate and make special arrangements for me!'

'What the fuck are you talking about?'

I realized that Kath had not told him; that he was phoning for some reason of his own. 'I've just been diagnosed with brain cancer,' I told him, biting the words off. 'I'm going to *die*, and I don't want to spend my last months on earth doing public relations for a sleazy company like MHD.'

There was a long silence. I reached Canalside and went into the lobby.

'You're . . . Is this *true*?'

'You want to talk to my doctor? His name's Hillman, a consultant neurologist. Phone him if you like. I'll get him to send you all the appropriate forms when I see him on Monday. If MHD tries to contest this, Ken, you'll get *slaughtered*.'

'I . . . I . . . You have *brain cancer*?'

'Yes. The prognosis is six months, max. What was it you phoned me about?'

'I . . . Those reports you left with me last night, I . . .' He was plaintive now. 'I didn't see why you'd given me all that old stuff to look at *now*, and I thought if you were going to dump a whole load of things in my in-box you should be around to *help*. Your PA said you'd phoned in sick, but I called you at home, and you weren't in. I . . . I thought you were malingering.'

'Oh, did you?' My head was throbbing.

'I, uh, misunderstood. I never thought . . . I didn't realize . . . You seemed perfectly fine yesterday.'

'You knew I was having tests though.'

'Well, yes, but . . . but it was an understandable mistake.'

'And of course it's also understandable that you had to start off by swearing at me.'

'You don't have to be like that! I apologized!'

'Actually, you know, Ken, you didn't. You simply excused yourself and decided it was an understandable mistake. All your mistakes are understandable. Now that I come to think of it, I don't believe I've ever heard you or any other MHD executive apologize to anyone. When people get hurt, it always turns out that it was in no way *your* fault.'

'You've got no right to lecture me!'

'Then I won't.' I cut the call.

Back in the flat I took two co-codamols and lay down with a damp washcloth over my eyes. Everything was quiet. The pain in my head pulsed in synchrony with my heart, fading slowly as the painkillers kicked in.

After a while I sat up and went to check my print-outs.

They were still there, sitting beside my computer, looking innocuous. The story they evidenced was also in *no way* MHD's fault.

It's actually rather unusual for a furniture company to *know* where its timber comes from. They usually buy from importers, who buy from dealers, who buy from sawmills, who deal with both reputable and disreputable loggers. Unless the chain of supply is controlled, plantation and illegally logged rainforest wood are hopelessly intermingled from the moment they're cut. Masterpiece Home Design, however, was actually a daughter company, a subsidiary of ABC Holdings, a multi-national based in Hong Kong. ABC ran a number of other furniture companies, in various nations, and also dealt in timber and paper. Sulong Logging, another subsidiary of ABC, cut quality timber in Malaysia. In the incestuous fashion of multi-nationals, it was a major supplier of Asian hardwoods to MHD and its sisters. The supply chain was short and unambiguous.

Sarawak is the larger of the two Malaysian states on the island of Borneo; much of it is still covered by a rainforest the size of Austria. Sulong and its kind have hit it hard. They are not careful stewards of their resources: they knock down six trees with bulldozers for every one they attack with chain-saws, and they've destroyed so much forest that production is dropping, not because of the Malaysian government's inter-mittant conservation efforts, but because they're running out of trees. The steep hills, once cleared of forest, erode quickly in the tropical downpours, filling the rivers with silt. Palm oil plantations, planted in the wake of forest clearance, add pollutants.

Much of the logging is illegal. Malaysia has signed up to most of the conventions on biodiversity and conservation; it has a developing tourism industry, in aid of which it has established large national parks, where eager Westerners can hope for a glimpse of an orangutan or proboscis monkey. In practice the Malaysian government tends to be at best half-hearted about conservation – but it is at least an issue. The timber trade, however, is worth *billions*. The companies engaged in it tend to have government ministers on the board and large numbers of thugs on the ground, and they flout the law on a regular basis.

Sarawak has a number of indigenous people, including some who used to be nomadic hunter-gatherers but who are now mostly semi settled. Until recently they relied to a large extent on the forest for sustenance, and the destruction of the forest has hit them hard. They can't find game or food plants; the silt-filled rivers are short of fish, and the pollu-tion gives them diseases of the skin and stomach. Many of them are reduced to working on the palm oil plantations, where they do heavy labour for miserable pay and are routinely treated with contempt by more successful ethnic groups. Needless to say, they are opposed to logging.

One group of indigenous people, the Penan, started a campaign, setting up barricades on the loggers' access roads and taking legal action, with the assistance of Malaysian and foreign conservation groups. The loggers responded with threats, and appealed to their parent companies for help.

ABC Holdings' daughter companies had orders for

furniture or timber products for which they needed the contested logs. They were indignant at the sudden shortages and subsequent loss of revenue and customers. They all contributed to a war chest – a substantial sum officially to be used for fighting legal actions and, unofficially, for bribes and dirty tricks.

They did not, of course, intend the massacre of thirty-eight inhabitants of a Penan settlement which had been constructing barricades in the Magoh River area. Nor, of course, did they *order* anyone to shoot the three activists and the lawyer in Sarawak's regional capital, Kuching. Orders were exceeded; things got out of hand. It wasn't their fault.

If you deal with a company known to ride roughshod over local law, which has been caught threatening villagers that it will 'come and kill your children' if they don't stop their obstruction; if you give such a company a large sum of money and tell them you need thirty thousand tons of timber *next week*, and you don't care how they get it, then *obviously* it isn't your fault if they proceed to break the law. You never meant that. You certainly never meant them to *kill* anybody.

Particularly not the three-year-old boy found hacked to death with a machete.

The story never made it into the Western media: none of the people killed were Westerners. I'd only heard about it because the conservation pressure groups, who had identified MHD as a leading retailer of tropical hardwoods, had bombarded me with it. They'd had pictures: the bodies in the street of Kuching, with anxious Malaysian police trying to shoo away the gawpers; the other bodies, huddled in their huts or sprawled beside their firepits; the little boy, dead and half-dismembered beside the bloody corpse of his mother. She'd been wearing a T-shirt with a picture of a hornbill on it and the logo of an environmental charity. He had worn only a loincloth.

Nobody had been prosecuted for the murders. A couple of thugs who worked for Sulong Logging had been arrested, but released again 'for lack of evidence' amid rumours of bribery and intimidation. Sulong Logging was still in business. MHD was still buying from it.

I read through my print-outs yet again. The two 'Magoh

River' files were emails from Alfred Howarth, CEO of MHD, to ABC Holdings, c/c Sulong Logging – the same stately, white-haired gentleman who smiled so nicely in our promotional literature. The first complained about the absence of a promised shipment of timber. *We are aware that the Penan blockade has interrupted the supply,* said Mr Howarth, *but similar problems have been dealt with in the past. It is surely past time for Sulong Logging to take firm action. The delays are damaging our reputation and costing us custom.*

The second letter had been written a couple of weeks later, after the massacre. *Sulong must spare no effort to clear itself. Evidence of connection between our company and the perpetrators of this atrocity would be extremely damaging to us.*

The 'Sulong Logging' file detailed the transfers of money. The last one had been made on the same date as the second email – after the massacre, when Sulong needed money to get itself off the hook.

Had MHD broken the law? Probably not: the company could always claim to *believe* that its suppliers were innocent. The evidence was, nonetheless, quite enough to damn it in the eyes of the public. The question was who I should take it to. Any of the conservation groups who had previously bombarded me would be interested – Friends of the Earth, Greenpeace, Rainforestweb. I felt, though, that it might be better to turn to a smaller group which had more direct links with Southeast Asia. The c/c email to Sulong Logging was addressed to named individuals, and the money transfers specified particular accounts. Somebody in Malaysia might be able to use that information.

I set the print-outs down, switched on my computer, and began searching through my contacts folder for a pressure group I half-remembered.

Scots Pine
Pinus Sylvestris
Britain and Northern Europe

Abundant

Three

I went to see the Southeast Asian Rainforests Trust on Monday, taking the print-outs with me in a crisp white envelope. I could have just emailed them, of course, but I wanted the satisfaction of actually setting the documents in human hands, and the Trust had an office locally.

The office was, predictably, in the university area, and I had misgivings the moment I saw it. It was a narrow slot in a terrace of shops, squeezed between a Turkish takeaway and a British Heart Foundation charity shop. Its window displayed a poster of an orangutan and some old crockery, along with a notice: 'Books, CDs, bric-a-brac only, please. We are sorry but we no longer take clothing.'

Inside it was, indeed, a charity shop, with a rack of CDs on one side of the narrow little room, a bookshelf on the other, and a table covered with old cutlery and glassware in the middle. A woman in a white headscarf was crouched over a box of second-hand paperbacks, arranging them on the shelf. She looked round as I came in, a young, brown face with large round spectacles. The headscarf was one of those long ones that wrap around under the chin and leave the face stranded. She stood up, and I saw she was wearing one of those shapeless long tunics on top of baggy jeans. 'May I help you?' she asked politely. She had an accent, not quite Indian but similar.

'My name is Antonia Lanchester,' I told her. 'I'm here to see Thomas Holden. I phoned earlier.'

She looked at me, clearly bemused. 'I'm sorry, he did not tell me you were coming.'

'I'm sure he expects me. Where's his office, please?'

She looked embarrassed. 'I'm sorry, he has gone out. If you wait, I will get you some coffee.'

I was in no hurry, but I was still annoyed. I'd *spoken* to Thomas Holden only about an hour before, and he'd given no indication that he was about to go out. I let the young Muslim woman lead me to a pokey office behind the shop. The walls were covered in pictures of orchids, hornbills, orangs and birds of paradise; the laptop on the cheap pine desk was almost submerged under a pile of papers, magazines, and used coffee mugs. The young woman picked up the electric kettle that sat on the floor, sloshed it to check for water, then set it down again and switched it on. She offered me the desk chair, which was the only seat in the room.

I sat gingerly on the grubby polyester. 'Did Thomas Holden say when he'd be back?'

'I'm sorry, he did not.'

There was a silence. The girl looked about, excavated a couple of coffee mugs from the desk, made a face, and took them out through a further door into what was evidently a restroom, because I heard the water come on as she washed them. I looked at Thomas Holden's desk, then picked up the nearest pamphlet. It was headed NGOs CONDEMN MALAYSIAN GOVERNMENT FORESTRY CERTIFICATION SCHEME, and contained three pages of dense type, setting out the reasons why. I didn't see it doing much to stir up the masses. I didn't see this organization doing so, either.

The girl came back with the clean mugs. 'Look,' I told her. 'Don't bother. I'll just go.'

She blinked at me, owlish behind the spectacles. 'I'm sure he will be back very soon.'

On cue, the door banged, and in walked two men, one in jeans and the other in a suit.

'Ah!' said the one in jeans triumphantly. 'Ms Lanchester, I presume!'

His tone was immensely irritating, but I got to my feet and offered my hand. 'Mr Holden?'

He ignored the hand. 'This is Rafik Nawaz,' he said, indicating the man in the suit. 'He's a lawyer. I thought I recognized your name, see, and I checked. You're PR officer for Masterpiece Home Design.'

Horrified gasps: the villain is unmasked! 'So I am,' I said

pleasantly. 'And, frustrated by your foresight in seeing fit to bring along your lawyer, I will retreat from the scene, gnashing my teeth. Goodbye, Mr Holden.'

I would have walked out, but he and Nawaz were standing in the door, clearly taken aback. 'What did you want to see me about?' asked Thomas Holden, now much less sure of himself. He was twenty-five or thereabouts, with curly brown hair and blue eyes, not bad-looking. Nawaz, an amused young Asian, was about the same age, and I suspected that Holden had roped in an old school friend.

'You can forget it. I've changed my mind.'

'This isn't about that article for Friends of the Earth?'

'No. Did you write one?'

'Well – yes. I thought . . .'

'It obviously didn't make as much of a splash as you'd hoped – and, actually, you know, companies don't usually send their PR directors as the bearers of writs. Please will you get out of the way?'

'So what did you want?'

'I told you, I changed my mind. Forget I came. Please?' I indicated the direction I wanted to go, and he moved out of the way.

'She came to give you that envelope!' exclaimed the young Muslim woman suddenly. 'That is the reason, isn't it?'

I had the envelope in plain sight, of course: it was too big to fit into a handbag. Everyone in the room now looked at it.

'It is information!' said the girl excitedly. 'It is a gift!'

'I'm sorry if I offended you,' said Thomas Holden slowly. 'I think I misunderstood the situation.' He looked like he was beginning to grasp it.

'And it was a *totally understandable* mistake,' I replied sourly. 'Look, I'm not leaving because I'm offended; I'm leaving because I had a mistaken idea about what the Asian Rainforests Trust actually was. Your website is quite professional, and you'd emailed me a lot in the past. I expected something rather larger and better equipped. I'll take this to one of the more established campaigns, OK?'

'They actually *are* quite professional,' volunteered Nawaz the lawyer helpfully. His accent was Midlands, like Holden's.

'It's just that most of their organization is in Indonesia and Malaysia. All Tom does is run the website and help coordinate things.' He smiled. 'They wanted somebody overseas to coordinate. Their offices in Southeast Asia keep getting shut down.'

I hesitated.

'There must be some reason why you didn't start off with one of the more established campaigns,' Nawaz coaxed.

'I wanted somebody with direct links to Southeast Asia,' I admitted. I hesitated some more, looking from one of them to the other, then took the plunge. 'You know about the Magoh River massacre?'

Behind me the Muslim girl exclaimed. 'Ah!' It was a very soft exclamation, but the feeling in it was electrifying.

'This is . . . to do with that.' I laid the envelope carefully on top of the pamphlets on Holden's desk.

The Muslim girl swiftly stepped over and picked it up. She held it in both hands and stared at it without opening it, her face both solemn and excited.

'It doesn't prove criminal wrongdoing on the part of my employers,' I warned them all. 'But there's some financial information which I hope somebody in Malaysia could use to – I don't know – trace payments or something.'

The girl turned her face toward me and beamed. 'Mrs Lanchester, I thank you, very much I thank you! I have prayed to God for this. God is great!'

'Ms Lanchester, thank you,' Holden repeated breathlessly, going over to the girl and taking the envelope, then glancing back at me. 'Are you going to get into trouble for this? Rafi, is she going to get into trouble?'

Nawaz shrugged. 'Depends whether it's breach of contract or just breach of confidence. Her employers aren't going to be happy, though, whatever the legalities. From what you've told me, they've spent a lot of effort denying they know anything whatsoever about the source of their timber.'

'They're my *ex*-employers,' I informed him with satisfaction. 'I resigned last Friday. I should warn you, though, I shouldn't even have *seen* that information, let alone passed it on. I got it from my boss's computer one night after he'd gone home.'

Nawaz looked uneasy. 'They might be able to prosecute for that.'

'So she should apply for protection as a whistleblower?' asked Holden.

'Don't know that she *could*, if there's no evidence of criminal wrongdoing in the UK.' Nawaz shrugged. 'Of course, if they're sensible they'll decide that prosecution would just draw more attention to the matter – but you can't rely on corporations being sensible.'

'Could they prosecute you for publishing?' I asked. 'Or just me, for stealing?'

The question took him aback. 'Just you.'

'How long would it take for the case to come to court?'

He was startled. 'Depends on whether it'd go to County or High Court. Civil cases are always slow, though. Six months to a year, maybe? '

I smirked. 'Well, then, I'm safe. I've been told I have less than six months to live. I wish you all joy of the information, and every success in your campaigns. Take care.'

I sailed out of the dingy office, leaving them gaping after me.

I had driven to their office, appeasing my reproachful conscience by telling myself that it would be the last time. I drove the Porsche home again and parked it. When I went to the hospital for my appointment at two, I took the bus.

Dr Hillman was much changed from our first meetings: he was now considerate, courteous, and not the least bit smug. He had already arranged for the second opinion – a consultant neurologist in the next town, whom I could visit or telephone, whichever I preferred. He'd put my name down for the biopsy, and hoped I would get a date for the operation within the next two weeks. He agreed with my decision to stop work at once, and was happy to provide a statement of my condition for my employers. He discussed the dexamethasone – which had turned out to be a steroid with a fearsome list of potential side-effects – and agreed that if the side-effects materialized I could telephone for an alternative. He explained astrocytomas to me again, and asked if I had any questions.

I hesitated, then ventured, 'I think I had a hallucination the other day. Is that going to happen again?'

'Ah.' He looked uncomfortable. 'Um. A, uh, hallucination?'

'I saw my furniture dripping blood.'

'Oh.' There was a silence. 'Well. You know that this tumour is causing disruption to the functioning of your brain, particularly to your right temporal lobe and your visual cortex. Any disruption of the visual cortex can cause visual hallucinations: it's a recognized effect. The temporal lobe . . . It's less clear-cut in what it does, but it seems to be involved in processing memories and in assigning significance to events.'

'You're saying that my brain was trying to show me something significant?'

'That's an unduly *purposeful* way of interpreting it. Your brain is under stress, and is producing images of things to which you *attach* significance. If they're . . . disturbing, you simply need to remind yourself that it's a natural phenomenon and that it isn't real.'

'So it *is* likely to happen again?'

He looked uncomfortable. 'One can't be sure, but yes, given that it's happened once, it's likely to happen again. I hope you're following my advice and have stopped driving.'

I took the bus home. It was half past three, and at first the bus was almost empty. A few older primary-school children got on outside a school, and began discussing a Halloween party loudly, with occasional shrill shrieks of derision or excitement. I was half-listening to them and half-wondering what I should do next when I saw the child.

He was tiny, brown-skinned and black-haired, and his bare arms and torso were streaked with blood. At first I thought he was something to do with the Halloween festivities – but he was too young, not old enough to be in school yet, let alone old enough to be travelling on a bus on his own, half-naked and untouched by the October cold. He glanced around the bus, and then his eyes fixed on me. He came down the aisle toward me eagerly, balancing easily on his bare feet. The dark eyes regarded me with hope and trust. I watched his approach, paralysed – then told myself that he wasn't real. A natural phenomenon, a false creation, proceeding from my heat-oppressed brain. Knowing it, I still couldn't stop myself from smiling back when he came up to me with a shy smile and extended his little hand.

''Scuse me,' said someone, and I looked up and saw that it was the bus driver. I looked back: the child was gone. What was more, the bus was empty and motionless, the engine switched off. I glanced about. It had pulled in at the stand in the main bus depot. My head began to ache fiercely and my stomach heaved.

'Are you all right?' asked the bus driver.

'I . . .' I swallowed. 'I was daydreaming. I was supposed to get off at Park Street.'

He made a non-committal noise. 'Well, you'll have to catch another bus back. I'm going off duty, and I'm supposed to leave the vehicle locked.'

I stumbled out, found the right bus stop, and stood in the queue. My head was pounding, and I leaned heavily against the guide rail, then, as misery overcame embarrassment, sat down on the bare floor with my head against my knees. The others in the queue stared at me suspiciously. Is this woman drunk? Drugged?

The bus came in the end, and lurched back into town. When I finally got off at Park Street it was five in the evening. It was dark, and it had started to rain. I walked home from the bus stop, head throbbing, hands thrust deep into the pockets of my wet coat, cursing hallucinations and public transport.

When I finally made it back to the flat, I found that a bouquet of flowers had been delivered in my absence. They sat outside the door, a thick mass of freesias, jasmine and ferns. I was afraid it was another hallucination, and I stared at it as though it would sprout legs and scuttle off. When it didn't, I gingerly bent to inspect it, and found the card.

Dear Toni, it said, in a florist's cod-copperplate italics, *so very sorry to hear your dreadful news. Please come back in, at least to say goodbye. Kath, and all at MHD.*

I had no doubt that the flowers had been Kath's idea, and that she'd ordered and paid for them herself; I didn't see Ken thinking of them. I hoped she would at least chase up some of the others for a contribution. I scooped up the bouquet, took it inside, and stuck it in a vase, which I set on top of the sideboard. Then I took a couple of co-codamols and lay down for a bit.

I made myself supper, taking more time over it than usual, and I opened a bottle of decent wine. When the food was ready, I lit a couple of candles and arranged them on either side of the flowers. I put on some music – Schubert's 'Trout' Quintet – and sat down on the sofa to enjoy my evening.

It didn't work: the satisfaction of delivering the print-outs had worn off, and the horror of what lay before me was overwhelming. I felt as though I was watching an accident in slow motion – seeing the building start to fall, the oncoming car bearing down, the edge of the cliff ahead – unable to do anything to escape. The smoked salmon linguine was dust and ashes in my mouth; the white Rioja was gall.

I had asked myself what I wanted to do with my last months on earth, then I'd done it. What now? Go on that round-the-world cruise, alone?

I stared at the candles, and tried to remember when I'd last eaten a candlelit dinner in company.

There had been a journalist, David something-or-other, some time in the summer. I'd met him over publicity for furniture, gone out with him a few times, had him to dinner once. I hadn't gone to bed with him, which he seemed to take offence at – at any rate, he'd stopped returning my calls. Before that there had been Will, another journalist, for about two months, until I got sick of his laziness and his self-obsession. Before that it had been . . . Ian. My ex. Another lazy, self-obsessed son of a bitch: I seemed to fall for them in haste and repent at leisure.

I saw him on the television sometimes, usually in thrillers. There had been one recently where he'd played a dodgy journalist, wheedling the truth out of a nervous civil servant, charming her as thoroughly as he'd charmed me, and just as disastrously. They'd both died for it at the end of Part One.

He had disdained television when we were married. *Live theatre*, he'd said, *was the only real acting*. Easy to insist on it, when he had a wife willing to work all hours to support him.

I thought about phoning Ian and saying . . . what? 'Hello,

how are you? Oh, me, I've got brain cancer and I'll be dead within six months . . .'

Wouldn't work: he'd be too busy telling me about himself to *ask* how I was. To be fair, he'd assume I was fine. He assumed everyone and everything was just fine, until its not-fineness jumped out and bit him. The divorce had come as a complete surprise to him.

I wished, nonetheless, that he was *there*, that I could snuggle up to him and hide my face in his wide shoulder; that he would put his arm around my waist and stroke my hair and kiss me, so gently . . .

I was going to die alone. I pushed my plate aside and began to cry again, tears of self-pity and grievous loss. It made my head ache, though, so eventually I stopped.

Well, what was I to do? Go searching for old boyfriends to make peace, like some character in a play? The thought of their horror at my news, their pity, their – I had no doubt at all – awkward, guilty retreat, was repellant. No, I would not call on any of them. I would send Ian a letter informing him of the news – a formal, dignified letter, with no pleas for company or support. Not tonight, though. Some time when I was feeling stronger.

It was infuriating. I had no idea what to do with myself that evening. You would think that when your days are numbered, you'd find a thousand things you want to do, but I was too shattered to think of even one. I was not tired enough to sleep, but far too tired and overwrought to take on anything practical. My head hurt too much to let me watch television or read, and anyway I couldn't concentrate. In the end I put on some opera and listened to it with a cold cloth over my eyes, for hours, until it was late enough to go to bed.

The next couple of days passed with terrible slowness. I got the pension fund forms, filled them in, and sent them off. I set up an account with an internet grocery delivery service, so that I could do the shopping without being able to drive. I made a half-hearted start on clearing out the cupboards. I telephoned the second-opinion doctor, and was not surprised to find that he agreed entirely with the first one.

Joanna from MHD's personnel office phoned, saying that they'd received my letter of resignation and the statement from Dr Hillman, but that they still wanted me to come into the office again, 'to sort out details' and 'tie up loose ends'. She was at least polite.

I told her that I'd need to arrange a time. 'I've been told not to drive,' I informed her coolly, 'so I'll have to book transport. I have a lot of other business to sort out, too. I'll get back to you, shall I?'

Joanna from Personnel would not normally accept such a limp evasion – but, faced with a dying woman, she could only hem and haw and say it would be fine.

The hospital also telephoned to say that the biopsy had been scheduled for the following Tuesday. It could be done under a local anaesthetic, they said, but I would have to stay in overnight – or longer, if I had no one to help me at home.

I was sitting at the computer on Thursday morning, gritting my teeth while forcing myself to plan a holiday, when the doorbell rang.

I went to the intercom panel by the door – the flats were supposed to be residents-only, though delivery people seemed to have no trouble getting in – and pressed the button. 'Yes?'

'Mrs Lanchester?' said a young, foreign, female voice. 'I am Nur Rashidah Aziz; I met you Monday, at the Rainforest Trust. Please may I speak with you?'

'How did you get my home address?' I demanded suspiciously.

'From Masterpiece Home Design. I said I had found a letter addressed to you, and they said I should send it here. Please? I wish very much to speak to you.'

I sighed, then pressed the button to open the street door.

A minute later she was knocking on the door of my flat. She was wearing the same headscarf, the same owlish specs and shapeless tunic; the bright colours of the Tesco shopping bag she was carrying stood out in sharp contrast. She gave me a nervous smile, and I stood aside to let her in.

Inside the flat, she stood looking about uncertainly. I offered her tea or coffee, and she thanked me and asked for tea. She took it black, with sugar. When I addressed her as

'Ms Aziz', she told me to call her Nur Rashidah. I did not respond with permission to call me Antonia.

Seated on the sofa, she set the tea down on the occasional table and hauled something out of the Tesco bag. It was, I saw, a photo album.

'Mrs Lanchester,' she said earnestly, 'I am very grateful to you for bringing us those documents. I wanted to thank you again. I brought this, to show you. You see . . .' She opened the album and flipped through several pages, then set it down carefully on the empty bit of sofa between us. The picture she'd selected seemed to be some kind of family portrait: besuited paterfamilias; stout materfamilias in a white headscarf and flowery dress; two smart young men in suits; a pretty girl in a headscarf and trouser suit. 'That is my aunt,' said Nur Rashidah, pointing at the woman. 'And this, this is my cousin Abdul.' She pointed at one of the young men.

Cousin Abdul had slicked-back hair and a white-toothed grin. His mother was resting a proud hand on his shoulder.

'Abdul was a lawyer,' the girl went on. 'God gave him a great love of justice and compassion for the poor. He got work with an environmental group that campaigns for the preservation of the forest and tries to help the people of the forest protect their lands. He was murdered last year.'

'Oh.' I looked at Cousin Abdul again, and thought of the pictures I'd seen – the bodies lying sprawled in the street, with the frightened Malaysian police trying to shoo the cameras away.

'The police think that he was killed because he was helping the Penan people, but they have not caught his murderer. It has been a year, and they've made no progress. My uncle used to phone them and shout at them, but now they've got an injunction to stop him. My aunt is sick with grief, she is afraid all the time. Whenever my other cousins leave the house, she is always phoning them and wanting to know where they are.'

'I'm very sorry.'

Nur Rashidah looked up at me, light reflecting off her specs. 'No, no! You have helped us. We have emailed copies of your documents to a coalition of environmental groups in Sabah and Sarawak – the Rainforest Trust is a member, it helps them coordinate. I hope that now we can bring the evil men who killed Abdul to justice. I wanted you to know that.'

'Well . . . thank you.' I felt overwhelmed. After a moment I managed to say, 'Is that why you're working for the Rainforest Trust? Because of your cousin?' The astounding coincidence that her family was actually *connected* to the massacre probably wasn't so astounding when you analysed it. I'd chosen the Rainforest Trust because, out of all the charities and pressure groups I knew, it was the one most likely to have a connection to the massacre. Nur Rashidah had probably chosen it for exactly the same reason.

She nodded solemnly. 'My cousin became a martyr because he helped the poor people of the forest. I wanted to do something to help them too.' Then she looked down and added, 'But I am only there part-time, as a volunteer. I am in Britain as a student.'

'Oh, really? At the university? What are you studying?' It was a relief to get away from this talk of justice and martyrs.

'Microbiology,' Nur Rashidah replied. As soon as she said it, I nodded. Yes, this solemn bespectacled girl would be studying something *factual* and *practical*.

Before I could ask her about how she liked the university, however, she went back to her main theme. 'When you came to the Rainforest Trust, Mrs Lanchester, you said a very sad thing, a thing that has weighed on my heart ever since. You said that you were ill, that you were going to die in six months . . .'

'Yes,' I agreed uncomfortably, 'I've been told I have an inoperable cancer of the brain.'

She didn't look away, which I liked: she met my eyes very directly, serious and unafraid. 'God is great and compassionate,' she said. 'To Him belong the darkness and the light. Mrs Lanchester, you have helped my family. I would like to help you, if you will permit.' Then she did look down, embarrassed. 'I do not know what kind of help you need, but I thought, if you are ill, there must be something. I could do the cleaning, or the shopping, or—'

'Thank you,' I interrupted her, 'but I have a cleaning lady and a grocery-delivery service.'

She looked up again. 'I would like to help!'

'Yes, I understand, and it's very kind of you. However, I don't really need help, at present – and I'm planning to go away for a bit, a couple of weeks from now.' Her talk of God made me nervous: I had no desire whatsoever to spend my last months fending off attempts to convert me to Islam.

'Oh.' After a moment she said timidly, 'I can drive. If you need someone to drive for you, I could do that.'

That was actually quite tempting, after my experience with the bus. I hadn't yet brought myself to advertise the Porsche for sale. 'You've driven in Britain?'

She hesitated. 'Only a little, on trips with friends. Here in Britain I have only a bicycle. But I do have a driving licence. At home I drive my mother's car.'

Of course, I could always take taxis, but I knew that it would be much more hassle than having a regular driver. Their reliability and time-keeping would be patchy, and they'd never be willing to wait while I ran errands.

'I've been told that I shouldn't drive,' I admitted. 'I was going to sell the car . . . but I'm finding public transport a bit of a struggle. If you're really eager to do something to help, you could drive for me. I'd pay you.'

'Oh, no, Mrs Lanchester, you do not need to pay me!'

'I would much prefer to,' I declared firmly. This was going to be a professional relationship or nothing. 'And you're a student: students *always* need money.'

Nur Rashidah hesitated, then nodded, smiling, pleased to have found something she could do. 'You can telephone me when you need to go somewhere, and I will come on my bicycle,' she told me shyly. 'I will give you my phone numbers.'

Cedar
Cedrus
Three species, widely distributed

The most famous, *Cedrus libani*, the cedar of Lebanon, is
reduced to six stands of timber

Four

Since I now had a driver, I had no excuse not to go over to 'tie up loose ends' with Joanna from Personnel. True, I still felt queasy at the thought of going back to MHD, but I knew perfectly well that my uneasiness came from the knowledge that I'd betrayed them, and not from any real expectation of danger. It was stupid to give in to an irrational fear; I ought to get it over with. I suggested to Nur Rashidah that she take me over to MHD headquarters on Friday morning.

She looked acutely embarrassed and informed me that she had lectures then. She could skip them, but . . . was it possible to go in the afternoon, instead?

We went over to the MHD offices the following afternoon. Nur Rashidah brought a heavy backpack with her, and I looked at it askance.

'It is some work for my course,' she told me, embarrassed. 'I thought I could work while I was waiting for you. That is all right?'

For a moment my imagination conjured up Muslim eco-bombers, but I reined it in sharply. Yes, *of course* she could bring along her microbiology texts!

Nur Rashidah was a careful driver – too careful for my taste. She slowed at every junction, even when the light was green; she always paused to let other cars pull out; she drove ten miles below the speed limit. I was fretting impatiently before we'd gone two miles. When we finally pulled into the MHD drive I was ready to leap out of the Porsche, but she slowed again, looking up at the glass front of the building with disapproval.

'They are rich from the oppression of the poor!' she declared indignantly.

'They sell furniture,' I corrected her. 'Not *all* of it is made
with illegally sourced timber.'

'Then why do they need to sell illegally sourced timber
at all? They could live on the sale of what they get lawfully;
they do not *need* to buy timber stolen from the lands of poor
forest people!'

Three years' worth of PR experience opened my mouth
to say, *It isn't the responsibility of a furniture company to
certify timber; timber is a valuable national resource for the
countries that sell it. Why should we deny it to the Third
World when we use it ourselves? Wood is the ultimate 'green'
product, if produced in a sustainable way: it can even lead
to replanting of rainforest . . .*

I shut my mouth. All of that was perfectly true, but not
relevant to my erstwhile employers – and I was no longer
bound to defend them. 'They're greedy,' I said instead. 'Are
you going to park this car or not?'

She parked the Porsche – with a bit of movement to-
and-fro so that it was *exactly* lined up – and I climbed out.
Nur Rashidah gathered up her backpack and moved over
into the passenger seat: apparently she meant to do her
reading in the car park.

'Come inside!' I ordered impatiently. 'I don't know how
long this is going to take, and it's cold. I'll find you a place
to sit indoors.'

When we entered the foyer, the receptionist gave Nur
Rashidah a puzzled glance before fixing me with a look of
pity.

I gave her a false smile. 'Hi. I've come back to see Joanna
in Personnel.' I couldn't remember the receptionist's name,
and glanced surreptitiously at her badge. *Sandy.*

'Uh, yes, Ms Lanchester,' Sandy muttered uncomfortably.
'I'll tell Joanna you're here.' She picked up the phone and did
so, looking at me as though she wanted to say something. She
set the phone down again, however, without saying it.

'This is my driver, Miss Aziz,' I informed her briskly.
'She's going to wait for me; is there somewhere she can sit?'

'Your driver?'

'You know that I've been diagnosed with brain cancer?'

Sandy grimaced and looked away. Of course she knew:

that was why she was so uncomfortable. She was in her early twenties, glossy and fashionable. Death was a morbid, horrible subject that sane and healthy people decently ignored. My presence before her, under the shadow of those dark wings, disturbed her. *Look*, it whispered, *it can happen to anyone. It could happen to you.*

'I've been told I shouldn't drive,' I informed her, 'so I'm employing Miss Aziz to drive for me. She's a student. I'd like you to arrange for her to have a table or desk for her books.'

'Oh. Yes. A desk.' Sandy, flustered now, glanced around the foyer – which, of course, contained no desks other than her own.

Nur Rashidah gave her an appeasing smile. 'I do not need a desk. I will sit there, by the window. I will do my course-work and wait.'

I left her spreading out her textbooks on the chocolate-coloured upholstery of the seats in the foyer, and took the lift up to Personnel.

Joanna, a large and heavily made-up blonde, was ordinarily aggressively loud and extrovert, but she greeted me in a hushed voice, and squeezed my hand, gazing soulfully into my eyes. Everyone else in the office stared in fascinated pity, looking away quickly if they happened to catch my eyes.

Dr Hillman's statement had been accepted, and a Form had been produced. It wasn't a particularly appropriate Form, but I filled it out with a string of N/As, signed it, and handed it back. I would get my next month's salary, I was informed with pride, as though this were an act of generosity on MHD's part, rather than a contractual obligation. That, however, seemed to be the limit of my entitlements: there would be no retirement bonus, and I could not expect any of the usual Christmas or New Year productivity payments. My work-related pension contributions were caught up in a tangle of restrictions. Joanna wasn't sure whether they could be cashed in. 'I'll try to sort it out for you,' she promised.

I did not *need* the money – and given what I'd just done to MHD, I would've felt very uncomfortable if they'd suddenly turned generous and caring – but the hushed solicitousness, coupled with the meanness, was setting my teeth on edge. 'How long will it take?' I asked, pretending concern.

Joanna pursed her lips. 'A couple of months? I'll certainly be able to do it by January.'

'I hate to tell you this, but that might be too late.'

The look I got was frankly horrified.

'I have between two and six months,' I reminded her. 'Doesn't Dr Hillman say that in his report? I *was* hoping to splash out a bit while I still feel well enough to enjoy myself. Why's it going to take so long? My private pension scheme can get me the money next month.'

'I'll . . . see if I can hurry it up,' Joanna muttered guiltily.

'*Thank* you, Joanna.' I gave her a warm smile. 'I'd prefer not to spend my last months worrying about money.'

She squirmed, and I knew that I would never see any of that money.

That seemed to be about it as far as Personnel was concerned. Joanna told me that Kath had asked me to stop by in Public Relations, to sort out a few details, and she insisted on walking me down there.

I was not surprised to discover that Kath had organized a goodbye party. Many of my erstwhile colleagues were assembled in my old office, looking uncomfortable, and the polished cedarwood of my old desk was covered with a lace-effect plastic tablecloth on which were arranged cups of clear plastic and an array of bottles and cartons. Kath was in red and black today: red blouse, black skirt; red tights, black shoes; red-and-black belt, red-and-black earrings. Her coordination had gone further than usual, though: her dark eyes were red. She exclaimed when I came in and hurried over to hug me. 'Oh, Toni!' she cried, letting me go again. 'I'm so sorry!'

I was unexpectedly touched and at the same time *angry*. I tried to swallow the burst of rage; Kath was the last person to deserve it. 'Yes, well,' I muttered. 'Shit happens.'

'We wanted to say goodbye,' Kath told me tremulously.

The goodbye budget had stretched to crisps, mushroom vol-au-vents and a cake. The cake was an elaborate one, decorated with chocolate flakes and my name in piped icing. *Just* my name: presumably nobody had known what to add. 'Goodbye' would, in the circumstances, have been in bad taste. 'Good luck' was either pointless or a bad joke. The possibility that occurred to me – 'Happy Ending' – must have seemed to everyone else to be facetious and futile. On reflection, it seemed that to me, too.

I thanked Kath, thanked the assembled company, and accepted a weak vodka and cranberry juice and a slice of cake. People came up and shook my hand uncomfortably, telling me how sorry they were. They clearly had no idea what more to say, and I found I didn't, either. The staples of office conversations – minor crises and complaints, flirtations and gossip, power politics – all seemed unutterably petty. I stood there, vodka and cranberry in hand, like some Old Testament prophet, come to announce the Lord's judgement on a wicked and frivolous generation. *Remember, o Man, that you are dust.*

Kath asked me about my plans; I muttered about taking a holiday in the sun somewhere, once I'd recovered from the biopsy on Tuesday. The assembled company fell upon this with relief: it meant that holiday destinations were a legitimate topic. Australia, suggested Tom; no, the Seychelles, insisted Joanna; Dave from Marketing plumped for Phuket.

As the minutes limped by, I found myself increasingly angry. What right did Tom or Joanna have to be so healthy and vigorous – talking about *scuba-diving*, for God's sake! The insurers would certainly forbid me to do that, even if I felt well enough to try. It was unfair. These shallow idiots could expect another thirty or forty years of holidays and love affairs. They would raise children and grandchildren; I was going to die before the next season's daffodils. What had they ever done to deserve such luck?

I had just set my empty glass down and was preparing to excuse myself when the office door flew open, and there was Ken. His face was flushed and his eyes were feverishly bright. He ignored everyone else in the room and stalked over.

'What have you done?' he demanded hoarsely.

'Ken!' Kath smiled nervously. She must have invited him, but he didn't look like he'd come to say goodbye.

'She's leaked private files!' Ken exclaimed, turning to her. 'Files nobody should've seen!'

I felt an unexpected jolt of vindictive glee. I wanted to shout, *Yes, I did!* Ken, at least, was going to know I'd been alive. I had just enough sense, though, to reply 'What?' instead. Admit it publicly and I might spend my last months bogged down in litigation.

'My files! My *very sensitive* files! What did you do with them?'

'I have no idea what you're talking about,' I said blandly. The world seemed much brighter than it had moments before.

'You went up to my office last Thursday. I know you did; you left that heap of documents!'

'Yes?'

'You did it then, didn't you? Didn't you?'

'Ken, what are you *doing*?' protested Joanna in horror. 'Poor Toni is . . . has been diagnosed with . . .'

'She copied sensitive files from my computer and gave them to some stupid lunatic tree-huggers!'

There was an instantaneous recoil right round the room – shock and, yes, a kind of awe. They all knew at once that I was guilty as charged – and they were impressed. They could never have done such a thing: they had their careers to think of. I was an invulnerable superhero: my strength was as the strength of ten, because I had nothing to lose.

I still had no intention of admitting it in front of all of them. 'I don't know what you're talking about, Ken.'

He stared at me, his eyes white-rimmed. 'Do you know what you've done?' he demanded shrilly. 'You have to fucking die, so you're going to take me with you, is that it?'

'Isn't that just a *tad* melodramatic?'

'Oh, you bitch!' He stood for a moment, quivering, nostrils dilated. His trousers gaped under the loosened buckle of his belt, exposing an inch of maroon underwear.

I smiled. What an absurd, pathetic, blustering fool! 'Do yourself a favour, Ken: go buy some trousers that fit.'

He gave a wordless bellow of rage, snatched a glass off the desk, and hurled it at me. But it was only plastic and, hard as he threw it, the worst effect of the impact was that it spilled cranberry juice over my grey silk jacket and white shirt. I looked down at the splash in anger and disgust, and saw that my shoulder was covered with blood. I pressed my hand against the stain, shocked now, and frightened. Ken was looking at me strangely. His eyes were very black, the pupils dilated, and the hand that had thrown the cup was dripping red. Everything had gone very quiet, and I saw that the floor was covered with snow. The blood from Ken's hand dripped on to it, marking the whiteness with a constellation of red suns.

Not real, *not real*. I closed my eyes, struggling to draw breath. The pain in my head exploded behind the lids, flowering red, and I pressed my hands blindly against the sockets of my eyes.

'Toni?' came Kath's voice, close beside me.

I was afraid to open my eyes. 'I want to go home,' I told her thickly.

There was a moment of silence, and then a hand caught my arm. 'Sit down, sit down!' Kath ordered breathlessly. 'Get a chair for her. Toni, are you OK?'

Stupid thing to ask. Obviously, I wasn't.

'Oh, very convenient!' sneered Ken in angry disgust.

I wanted to laugh, but my head hurt too much. Someone else cried an angry reproach. Kath steered me to the left, and I felt a chair against my knees. I pushed it aside impatiently. I didn't want to be trapped in the snow with Ken and his blood-stained hands: I wanted to escape. 'I want to go home!' I repeated, pleading like a small child.

'I'll take you to hospital,' offered Kath, her voice frightened.

'No! Please, my driver is waiting in the foyer; she'll take me home.'

Kath capitulated and steered me out of the office. I heard the anxious discussion begin even as I stumbled out the door.

I risked opening my eyes when we were in the corridor: to my intense relief, the snow had gone.

When we reached the foyer Nur Rashidah came running over. 'What has happened?' she demanded in alarm.

Kath answered before I could. 'I think she had some kind of attack. Our boss made a scene and set it off. I think she should go to the hospital. Are you her driver?'

'I'm all right!' I was angry, at myself for needing help, and, irrationally, at Kath for providing it.

Nur Rashidah and Kath both looked at me with identical expressions of grave concern and total disbelief.

'There's nothing a hospital can do,' I said, more honestly. 'This isn't going to get better. They told me that already. I want to stay out of the damned hospital as much as I can, for as long as I can, OK?'

'I will take you home,' Nur Rashidah promised quietly. She went back to scoop up her microbiology texts, then hurried to the door of the building and held it open for me.

Kath telephoned that evening, wanting to know how I was, and if there was anything she could do to help. 'I thought, shopping or something,' she offered. I thanked her and refused, explaining about the delivery service.

'Well, let me know if there's anything,' she said, almost apologetically.

I very nearly thanked her and left it. My flat was very quiet that evening, though, and I was oppressed by the prospect of spending my remaining months alone in that silence. My family and my closest friends were far away, in other cities. Somehow none of the people I'd met since starting to work for MHD had become anything more than acquaintances. I had no work to go to now, nothing to give order to my days.

'Maybe you could come round for coffee some time,' I suggested. 'Or a drink after work? It would be a pity to lose touch.'

There was a moment's silence, and then she said, 'I'd love to!'

We agreed that she would come round for coffee the following Saturday.

A few minutes after she'd rung off, I had another phone call – a less welcome one.

'I need to talk to you,' Ken told me breathlessly.

'About what?'

'You know what it's about, you bitch! About what you did!'

'What did I do, Ken?'

'Oh, you bitch, you *bitch*!'

I cut him off. A few minutes later, however, the phone rang again. It was Ken again. I hung up.

My mobile rang. 'Look,' said Ken, 'will you just tell me—'

I switched off the phone.

The landline rang again. I let it ring for about a minute, then switched it off as well – it was a cordless one, with a switch on the handset. I sat listening to the silence, hot with indignation. What did Ken think we had to talk about? Even if I admitted what I'd done, what good would it do him? Did he expect me to say I was *sorry*? I wasn't; when I thought about what Nur Rashidah had told me, I was *proud*.

I took the phone book from its place at the end of the breakfast bar and checked what it had to say about nuisance calls. As I'd thought, there was a freephone number to dial in order to block calls from a specified number. I switched my phone back on, dialled it, and arranged to block all calls from Ken Norman.

A fusillade of bangs outside my window made me jump. Suddenly afraid, I sat frozen on the sofa, phone book still on my lap. There was another rattle of explosions, and then I remembered that it was nearly the fifth of November; the evenings were beginning to fill with fireworks and the scent of gunpowder. I went to the window, smiling, and was just in time to see a crimson fountain hanging above the canal. Fireworks, yes! Let Ken try and phone now, and he'd explode as harmlessly.

At about noon the next day, Saturday, the doorbell rang. I'd been working on a letter to Ian, my ex, and I welcomed the interruption – until I hit the intercom, and discovered that the caller was Ken.

'I need to talk to you,' he announced breathlessly.

I was unreasonably furious. I did not want to deal with this; I had enough to worry about. 'Go away!'

'The files you took. I need to know . . .'

'Oh, for God's sake!'

'Please! I *know* you took them. I just need to know . . .'

'If you think I stole your fucking files, go tell the police! Go ahead, prosecute and be damned!'

'You know I can't! Please, just tell me . . .'

'You ruined my suit yesterday, you know that? You ruined my grey silk suit and you nearly gave me a seizure, and now you turn up *here*, and expect me to let you in? No way!'

'Please! I . . . I'm sorry about the suit. Look, look I know you were asking about your pension contributions. I could help with that. And you must be due some kind of retirement bonus or something. I could . . .'

I almost laughed. 'You're trying to *bribe* me?'

'All you need to do is discuss the situation with me. That's all I want, just . . . just to *discuss* things.'

'We have nothing to discuss. My God, a *retirement bonus*, how pathetic! I'd have to spend it fast!'

'Then tell me what you *want!*'

'Ten more years of life!'

'It's not *my* fault you need them!'

'But it *is* your fault that your computer was full of compromising files, isn't it? Go *away*, Ken. Go away, or I'll call the police.'

'You bitch, you bitch! What did I ever do to you? You've fucking *destroyed* me, and I never did *anything!*'

I was quivering with anger now. 'You really think this is all about *you*? You really think I said to myself, "I'm dying, so I'll make trouble for Ken Norman"? Do you think those people who died did it to get at you, too?'

'That was nothing to do with me!'

'You knew it happened. You knew it might come out. You tried to make sure it didn't, and now you're calling me a bitch because I told the truth. *Murder* was OK by you, but whistleblowing, well, that's quite beyond the pale!'

'Self-righteous bitch!'

'Go complain to your lawyer. Go do what you please, but just go *away*. You're not coming in here, that's for sure!' I took my finger off the intercom button and went back to my computer. Let him stand in the street and swear: I wasn't listening any more.

On the computer screen, my letter stared at me:

Dear Ian,
I'm writing this to inform you that I've been diagnosed with terminal brain cancer. The prognosis is two to six months.
    I don't need help, and I'm not asking you for it.

> There's nothing anyone can do, anyway. This is simply
> for your information. Also, for your information, I'm
> leaving the estate, such as it is, to charity.

That was as far as I'd got, and now that I looked at it, it
seemed cold and spiteful. I deleted it, then sat staring at the
blank screen. I was shaking. I wondered if Ken had gone
away.

I had no view of the entrance to Canalside from my flat.
I could get one by looking out the window of the eleventh-
floor landing – but suppose he'd managed to get in, on the
heels of another resident, and I met him coming up?

The possibility jolted me with cold sickness, and I wondered
why. I'd never been afraid of Ken Norman: I thought he was
ridiculous. True, he was obviously very angry, and true, he
blamed me for destroying his career – but if all he could do
in the throes of rage was throw a plastic cup full of cranberry
juice, he could hardly be considered dangerous . . .

The thing I was really afraid of, I supposed, was that a
confrontation would trigger another hallucination. Those
things scared me. They seemed so *real*. I remembered Ken
standing in the snow with the blood dripping from his hand,
and I shuddered. The headaches seemed to follow the visions,
too, and they were horrid.

I sat for a moment, resting my face in my hands. I
needed to write the letter. I needed to telephone my
mother and my brother and break the news. I needed to
send an email around all my friends and acquaintances.
*Delete me from your address books and your Christmas
lists as of next year, because I won't be here any more.*
It was almost two weeks since I'd heard. I needed to let
people know.

But I still couldn't do it. I exited the computer program
and went over to switch the television on. I channel-hopped
a few times, stared irritably at an ad for spaghetti sauce, a
garden make-over, a children's cartoon, then switched the
box off again. I thought about going for a walk, but decided
I hadn't left enough time for Ken to have gone away. I went
over to my bookshelf and picked up a volume of poetry at
random. It was Housman.

Now hollow fires burn out to black,
And lights are guttering low:
Square your shoulders, lift your pack,
And leave your friends and go.

Oh, never fear, man, nought's to dread,
Look not left nor right:
In all the endless road you tread
There's nothing but the night.

I read it twice, then leafed through some of the other poems in the book. Housman was always writing about death; he even made fun of his taste for the subject. I wondered why his gloomy verses made me feel better. Because he saw so clearly that death is a universal ill?

There's nothing but the night. I wondered if that were true. The atheist sneers at the believer's hope of Heaven and calls it wishful thinking – but, surely, saying that death is only oblivion is equally wishful? Oblivion, after all, is an everlasting sleep, and who's afraid of sleep? It's the dread of something *after* death that transfixes the imagination with terror.

Nur Rashidah probably believed in Heaven, or Paradise, or whatever the Muslims call it. I wondered if she thought I would go to Hell. Believers often shy away from condemning their unbelieving acquaintances to everlasting torment, even if it's a tenet of their faith, yet see nothing peculiar in showing themselves more merciful than the God they worship as the fount of all compassion. I've always been an agnostic, myself.

I dug a sheet of paper out of the desk drawer and a pen out of my handbag. It had been years since I wrote any poetry, and I was rusty, but soon the skills started to come back. I went for a traditional form because I needed the discipline; I counted out stresses on my fingers, scribbled rhyme words into the margin, and eventually emerged with a sonnet.

We say that death's the end – but are we right?
We cannot fathom consciousness or time.
Who knows what visions in the brain define
the final dreadful instant of our sight?
Perhaps it lasts forever, like a star

collapsing to a point, a hole in space
whose singularity escapes Time's race:
what we are then is what we always are.
Perhaps there's nothing but the dark. Who knows?
We're born to face the shadow of our end
in ignorance that learning cannot mend.
Sleep is a guess, and Heaven a hope that grows
mushroom-like in darkness. All is night
till death itself arrives, as dark or light.

No, it wasn't very good. Set beside the Housman, it was feeble indeed. I've never been a very good poet, though I once wanted to be, more than anything. I lack, always, that leap into the hard incandescence of inspiration. Still, somehow the effort of setting the words down in their strict pattern had trapped the horror. I was going to die – *abba* – but so was everybody else – *cddc*. It was the human condition – *effe gg*.

I wanted to live; I still wanted to live. But, in the end, no one can.

Walnut Veneer
Juglans regia
Balkans

Cultivated abundantly

Five

On Sunday I finally managed to telephone my mother and my brother. It was very unpleasant, though not quite as bad as I'd feared. My mother kept interrupting, trying desperately to find some hole through which she could extract hope. Maybe they'd got it wrong? Maybe the biopsy on Tuesday would overturn the verdict? My brother heard me in appalled silence and ended the call abruptly, saying he 'needed to take it in'. About an hour later, though, his wife phoned back to tell me about this wonderful detoxifying diet which helped people beat cancer; you had to drink fresh organic vegetable juice at regular intervals, and she thought there was a spa that could help with it. I told her it sounded like crap, and she rang off again in a huff.

I composed a couple of emails, too; one to friends and one to acquaintances, and despatched them into the ether. I felt, bizarrely, that I ought to attach some advice for the funeral. *No flowers, please. Donations to the Southeast Asian Rainforest Trust* or something like that – but I supposed my brother could do that in due course.

I wrote another letter to Ian, but once again deleted it without printing it out. I couldn't seem to get past the anger and disappointment that had ended our marriage, and I was ashamed to write from nothing else.

On Tuesday, Nur Rashidah drove me to the hospital for the biopsy.

I suppose it went well. There were no complications, anyway. I was given a local anaesthetic, and came away a bit later with a neatly shaved patch on the right side of my head and a bandage. The biopsy, however, revealed that the tumour was an 'astrocytic glioblastoma multiforme' – the most aggressive sort. Dr Hillman had warned me that I shouldn't hope, and I'd thought that I'd obeyed him, but I discovered that I hadn't when my last hope was extinguished.

Though pretty minimal, the procedure was still technically brain surgery. I felt very sick afterwards, and my head seemed to ache worse than ever. I hated the hospital – the ugliness of the metal-framed bed and grey lino, the smell of institutional food and disinfectant, the lack of privacy and quiet, the constant disturbances from nurses or other patients. Between bouts of helpless vomiting, I curled up in bed, wishing I were home.

Nur Rashidah turned up in the evening to visit. She'd brought a card with a picture of trees on it. It seemed that flowers were forbidden on grounds of hygiene. I thanked her listlessly.

After she left I lay quietly staring at the card. It must have been produced by the Rainforest Trust, or perhaps one of its partners, because the trees were tropical – huge things, with roots like flying buttresses. As I watched, a branch moved in the wind.

I picked the card up, staring, and suddenly the forest was all around me, the great grey trunks towering on either side, covering me with shadow. The sky was green with leaves. For once I was not frightened: the hallucination at least spared me the hospital. I lay quietly, staring upwards into the canopy, watching the shimmering of leaf on leaf, until I fell asleep.

I came home from the hospital next morning. The doctors didn't really approve, since I still hadn't been able to eat anything, but I was desperate to get away, and lied about how well I was feeling.

Nur Rashidah had doubts. 'You look very ill, Mrs Lanchester,' she told me on the way home. I probably did: I was slumped against the car window, staring fixedly at the road to keep my mind off the nausea. 'Are you sure you will be all right?'

'I'll be fine,' I insisted. 'I hate that place. If I stayed there, I'd never recover.'

We made our slow and cautious way back to Canalside. She parked the Porsche in its slot – with the usual backing to and fro – then helped me out of the car and supported me over to the lift. I thought about telling her she didn't need to, but in fact I was glad of her steady arm.

It was clear that something was wrong the moment we reached the flat. The lock panel on the door was scored, along with the door frame, and the door itself was dented. I pushed it, and it moved: the bolt had been broken.

I stopped there in the corridor, afraid to go in. Nur Rashidah looked at me anxiously. Ashamed of my cowardice, I gritted my teeth and opened the door.

The lounge looked like New Orleans after Hurricane Katrina. The two mahogany bookcases were empty, and my books lay scattered about the floor, some of them opened, with pages torn out. All my CDs had been tipped out on top of them, their jewel-bright plastic sleeves heaped on the iridescent circles like a smashed pane of stained glass. Even the DVDs had been hauled from their discreet hiding place in the cabinet under the television and piled on the carpet. The television itself had been thrown down on top of them: its case was dented, its screen cracked. The cream cushions had been thrown off the sofa and floated on the debris, icebergs on a sea of pages.

I leaned against the scarred door frame, swallowing bile. Nur Rashidah gave a little gasp, let go of my arm, and took a couple of hesitant steps into the room. She turned back to me, face full of pity. 'I am so sorry!'

I shook my head. I couldn't think of anything to say.

She looked unhappily round at the mess. 'You should lie down. You should lie down, and I will telephone the police.'

The bedroom, however, was no better than the lounge: all the drawers had been emptied, and my clothes lay in crumpled heaps on the carpet. Some of the more fragile items had been ripped in half. The mattress had been tipped off the bedframe and used to smash the bedside table; the pillows had been thrown into the bathtub and soaked. In the en-suite bathroom the cabinet was open, the contents of the drawers spilled in piles on the rust-coloured mat. I looked at the ruins, then went back into the lounge, stumbled over the books, and sat down heavily on the sofa.

'This is because of us,' Nur Rashidah declared guiltily. 'They were looking for the information you gave to us.'

I stared up at her, squinting against the headache. 'No, that's stupid! They know perfectly well that you've already *got* that information! People have been *using* it – that was clear from the way Ken was howling last Friday. The guys who did this must've been looking for money or jewellery.' I remembered abruptly that I'd left my credit cards, along with a stash of cash, in my desk drawer: the hospital had warned me not to bring in any valuables. I jumped to my feet, blundered across the rubble – a CD case cracked under my foot – and hurried into the spare room that I used as a study.

It had been treated the same way as the rest of the flat: books on the floor, files of household records tipped out on top of them. The desk drawers had been wrenched out of place and ripped open. One hung over the swivel chair, its walnut veneer dangling from the compressed hardboard body like a torn banner. The computer was gone. I went down on my knees and started to turn over the litter.

'Mrs Lanchester,' Nur Rashidah cried, and I looked round at her. 'Mrs Lanchester, please! You are very ill, you had *brain surgery* yesterday. You should lie down!'

'My credit cards,' I explained to her. 'I had them in the desk drawer.' When I wiped my nose I realized that I was starting to cry. I couldn't cope with this; I lacked the energy even to bear it, let alone clear up.

She glanced over the mess. 'You must lie down. I will telephone the police. Then I will look here for your credit cards, and if they are gone, you can telephone to stop them.'

I let her help me to my feet and guide me back into the lounge, treading on volumes of Shakespeare and discs of Monteverdi. I sat down on my ochre and gold sofa, snuffling. My head hurt, and I pressed my hands against my eyes, then took them away, suddenly wondering if this were another hallucination. I looked hopefully at Nur Rashidah, who was hovering anxiously.

'Am I seeing things?' I asked bluntly. 'Is my flat *really* in ruins?'

'I think it is not so bad as it seems, Mrs Lanchester,' she said earnestly. 'Most of your things are not broken. When they are back in order, it will all be beautiful again.'

No hallucination: this was reality. My home had been invaded, ransacked, trodden underfoot . . . like my brain. No, not like my brain. There was no way to tidy *that* up and make it beautiful again.

The tears overwhelmed me, and I slumped like a sand-castle at the turn of the tide. Nur Rashidah dithered a moment, then patted me on the shoulder, fetched me some tissues from the kitchen, and telephoned the police.

By the time the police arrived, I was lying down in bed. Nur Rashidah had hauled the mattress back on to the frame and remade the bed (using a cushion from the lounge inside a pillowcase and hanging the pillows over the shower screen to drip). She'd picked up the scattered clothing and stacked the undamaged items in a neat pile. This was after she'd searched the study and determined that my credit cards really weren't there, and I'd telephoned to cancel them.

The police had been in no hurry, which was good, because it meant I'd had time to calm down. By the time the door-bell rang, I'd regained my composure and was feeling ashamed of my breakdown. I got up and went to the intercom.

Nur Rashidah was hovering beside it, staring at the controls with doubt. She stepped aside gratefully to let me press the right button.

When the police had identified themselves and I'd pressed the button to unlock the building's door, I turned back to the lounge – and saw that Nur Rashidah had already begun tidying up. The CDs were stacked neatly beside the racks, the DVDs by the television, and the books were actually in the process of being reshelved.

'I did not want to leave it for you to do, when you are so ill,' she explained, seeing my look. 'I am putting the books in alphabetical order, is that right?'

'Should you have touched them at all, before the police got here?'

Her eyes widened, and she put a hand to her mouth in acute embarrassment. 'Oh! I am so stupid! Oh, I am *sorry*!'

I don't know why, but her embarrassment touched me where her kindness had left me cold. I hugged her, which was most unlike me, and surprised me when I thought about it afterward. 'Don't worry,' I told her thickly. 'You've been an *immense* help.'

The police didn't seem bothered that the scene of the crime had been tampered with. It was the fifth burgled property they'd visited that day, and it was only lunchtime. There were two of them, a man and a woman, both pleasant in a tired, disillusioned sort of way. They took statements from me and from Nur Rashidah as to how and when we'd discovered the break-in; they examined the debris; they asked, in a rather cursory way, about the building's security arrangements. The estate agent had waxed boastful about these when I bought the place, but the police didn't seem surprised that they'd been circumvented.

'It happens,' was the man's verdict. 'People leave the door wedged open because they're fetching in the groceries, and then forget to unwedge it – or they let in somebody who claims to have a delivery, or somebody who claims to be a friend of someone on another floor. Then the burglar does a quick recce to see who's home, and tries any room where nobody's collected the post, or any door that's unlocked. Had a university residence the other week where the guy hit twelve rooms in one go.'

None of the other inhabitants of Canalside had reported a burglary, however. I hadn't been away long enough for the post to have built up, and the shattered lock on my door proved that I'd left it secured. The police were mildly perplexed, and asked if I'd told many people that I'd be away.

'No,' I told them bluntly. 'Only my mother and my brother, and they don't even live in this city.' Then I thought about it, and added reluctantly, 'I suppose I might have mentioned it at the goodbye party at work last Friday.'

'What about you?' the policewoman asked Nur Rashidah.

'I told them at the Rainforest Trust, where I volunteer, that I could not come this morning because I needed to take Mrs Lanchester home from the hospital. I did not tell anyone when she went into the hospital, though . . . I do not *think* I told anyone that.'

The policewoman looked puzzled. 'Don't you live here?'

'Oh, no! I am a student at the university. I have a room in Elm Tree, one of the residences for international students.'

'Ah. I thought you were a lodger *here*. So what is your connection to Mrs Lanchester?'

I answered for her. 'She kindly offered to drive for me while I'm ill. When we saw that the flat had been burgled, she stayed to help.'

'Ah.' The policewoman bestowed on Nur Rashidah an approving, if still slightly puzzled smile. 'And she was picking you up from hospital? Nothing serious, I hope?'

'A biopsy,' I said forbiddingly.

'Please, there is one thing that troubles me very much,' Nur Rashidah interjected, her round, bespectacled face very serious. 'Last week Mrs Lanchester gave some information to the charity where I help – some information which is embarrassing to her employers. When I saw what happened here, I wondered if it was because of that.'

'What's this?' asked the policeman.

Damn. I'd wanted to keep quiet about what I'd done, to sidestep the trouble. 'I don't think this has anything to do with that!' I exclaimed.

'But whoever did this was searching for something!' Nur Rashidah pointed out. 'That is clear from the mess they made: they were searching. They came when they knew you would be away, and you say now that you had told people at Masterpiece Home Design when that would be. They did not take very much. I am surprised that they did not take the television or the music system.'

'They look for light, portable stuff,' replied the policeman. 'Money and jewellery. They don't want anything bulky, especially in a place like this, where they have to use a lift to get out of the building.'

'They took the computer.'

The policewoman just shrugged. 'Maybe they knew somebody who'd want it. What are you claiming?'

'Please, I am not *claiming* anything,' Nur Rashidah said hastily. 'I am worried, that is all.'

'What is she on about?' asked the policeman, turning to me.

I gritted my teeth. It seemed I was faced with a choice between explaining and telling a lie. 'Last week I blew the whistle on my employers,' I admitted, since it seemed better to avoid telling outright lies to the police. 'A company that's an associate of theirs is implicated in serious crimes in Malaysia, and I gave some information about it to the trust where Nur Rashidah volunteers. I don't see how this can be connected, though. I mean, it's *done* now.'

The policeman, however, was frowning. 'Any chance this could be a revenge attack?'

I opened my mouth, then remembered Ken shouting at me through the intercom, and shut it again. 'I don't know,' I admitted. 'My ex-boss *was* very angry about it. He phoned me until I blocked his number, and then he came here on Saturday and tried to get me to let him in. He shouted and swore when I wouldn't. He said I'd wrecked his career.' Even as I said it, I imagined Ken in my lounge, sweeping the books off the shelves and stamping on them, hurling down the television the way he'd hurled the glass of cranberry juice. I *could* imagine it, that was the unnerving thing; I could imagine it easily.

Both police officers were interested now. 'Your *ex*-boss?' asked the policewoman. 'You've had to resign?'

'I resigned on grounds of ill health, not . . . not because of the whistleblowing.'

'Still . . . What's the name of this ex-boss?'

I told them Ken's name and looked up his address for them. In response to their questions, I ended up telling them the whole story of the Magoh River massacre and Masterpiece Home Design's complicit silence. The police were interested, even excited, and promised to follow it up – although, as the policeman said, it was still probable that the burglary was totally unconnected, the work of someone motivated by nothing more exotic than greed or a drug habit. The pair dusted the CDs for fingerprints, left me an incident number for the insurers, and promised to ask the neighbours whether they'd noticed anything.

When they'd left, Nur Rashidah and I looked at one another. I thought about reproaching her for the way she'd put me on the spot with her precipitate accusation, then decided to say nothing. She'd been worried. It was possible that she'd been *right* to be worried. She didn't deserve reproach.

'What will you do now, Mrs Lanchester?' she asked. 'Shall I take you back to the hospital?'

I grimaced. 'No!'

Wherever I went, it wouldn't be there again, not until I was too ill for any alternative. I thought wistfully of how good it would have been to end the day lying in my own bed, listening to music. I looked wearily around my wrecked lounge. 'I'll see if I can book into a hotel. I don't want to stay here until the door's been fixed.' Belatedly, I thought to ask, 'Do you have somewhere you need to be this afternoon?'

'I have a lecture at two o'clock, but I can miss it.'

'No. No, you've given up enough of your time already. Go to your lecture. I'd appreciate it if you could drive me to the hotel, when I've found one, but I'll need some time to make phone calls and pack.'

I stayed at the Holiday Inn for two days. It was very restful, actually: I lay about on the king-sized bed, watching television and listening to Radio 3, eating takeaways or meals provided by room service, barely stirring from my room. I made numerous calls from my mobile – arranging cash and replacement credit cards; getting a man to fix the door of the flat; harrying the insurance people – but all of this seemed somehow less stressful from the perspective of a hotel bedroom than it would have done at home. Even when the credit card company contacted me with a query as to whether I'd spent £789.98 on a 'Sexsational Vibrating Lovebed' I was able to keep my composure and assure them that I had not, and that any credit-card purchase made after Monday was not mine. When Nur Rashidah drove me back to Canalside, Friday lunchtime, I was feeling much stronger.

I collected the new door key from my letterbox, along with a handful of mail, inspected and approved the new and more secure door to the flat – solid oak with steel hinges – and let myself back in.

The lounge was in the same dishevelled state as when I'd left it, but that was what I'd been expecting, and I could cope now. As Nur Rashidah had pointed out, most of the mess was disarray, not damage. Return everything to its place, and all would be restored to elegance. The television was a write-off, but the music centre, which I would have missed more, was untouched. I thanked Nur Rashidah for her help, assured her I didn't need any more of it just at the moment, said goodbye to her, then began the process of picking up and putting away.

When I'd sorted most of the lounge I sat down, drank a cup of tea, and went through the post.

There were several cards from people I'd emailed. A couple of them had sent Get Well cards, which annoyed and exasperated me. 'Hope you're back on your feet again soon'? Hadn't they *understood* what I'd told them? Did I have to spell it out? *I'm not going to be back on my feet, I'm going to be six feet under*?

I suspected that my email inbox held more of the irritating messages. I hadn't seen it since before the op: I didn't check it while I was in the hotel, and now I had no computer. I quailed at the thought of buying another and getting it set up, then told myself firmly that that would be my task for tomorrow, and that it wouldn't seem so intimidating then.

At the bottom of the stack of post was a letter – not an official one, as the address was handwritten in ink. I couldn't remember when I'd last received a personal letter. I supposed it was from one of my friends, wanting to send something less ephemeral than an email.

It wasn't.

Black biro on a sheet torn from a lined notepad:

DO YOU WANT TO DIE IN PEACE?
OR WILL YOUR LAST MONTHS BE HELL ON EARTH?
YOUR CHOICE.

I stared at this in consternation. Then the phone rang.

'Toni?' said Kath's breathless voice.

'Yes?'

'Oh, I'm so glad I finally got hold of you! Um. Are you OK?'

'Well, no worse.'

There was a silence, and then Kath said nervously, 'Do you . . . that is, have you seen Ken?'

I was obscurely alarmed. 'No. That is, he came round here last Saturday in a temper, but I didn't let him in. Why?'

'He hasn't come in to the office since Wednesday! Nobody knows where he is. They're saying the police have called, asking about him. I don't know what's going on. I . . . I've been trying to phone you; I thought you might know something, because of . . . you know . . .'

'You should've tried my mobile.'

'I did. It was always busy, but your home number just rang and rang! I couldn't work it out.'

'I've been in a hotel. Somebody broke into my flat on Tuesday and wrecked it. That's probably what the police want to talk to Ken about.'

'What? The police think *Ken* broke into—'

'I don't know! Somebody broke in and trashed the place, and the police asked if it could've been a revenge attack. They were planning to talk to Ken. He's missing?'

'He came in on Wednesday morning. He looked awful, though, and he went home at lunchtime. Toni, what *did* you take out of his computer? They're hiring in some really high-powered PR consultancy to take over here, and everybody's in a flap.'

I remembered that night with Ken's computer: the neon shadows on the wall, the rock and snow on the screen and the sense of a horror buried behind it. 'MHD has a link with a company that is widely believed to have killed some people in Malaysia,' I told Kath. 'They gave it money to help it break a blockade on logging roads, and then they gave it more money to help cover it up when persons unknown went too far and committed mass murder. I found two letters from our CEO, Mr Howarth, and a financial spreadsheet, which prove that they knew about the blockade and supported their supplier before and after the bloodshed. That's all.'

'Oh.' Kath sounded bewildered. 'Oh . . . MHD *killed*—'

'No. MHD supported an associated company which is suspected of involvement in killings. Nothing's been proved, and nobody *here* did anything criminal. Ken was over-reacting. I don't think any of this is going to be anything more than an embarrassment to MHD. I doubt it will even dent sales much. People who buy uncertified tropical hardwoods either don't know about the issue or have already decided to ignore it.'

'Oh. So why did you . . .?

'I was fed up with telling lies, Kath. I was just fed up with . . . with making excuses for the inexcusable, OK? People shouldn't *die* so that furniture companies can sell expensive hardwoods! I wanted to . . . I don't know, strike a blow for truth, or at least for a sense of proportion.'

'You really think Ken broke into your flat?'

'I don't know. He could have. You saw what he was like last week, how hysterical he was. It could've been just burglars, though.'

'I don't like this at all,' said Kath plaintively.

I sighed. 'I don't like it either. I'm sorry you're stuck with the results. I'm not sorry I did it.'

There was a silence, and then Kath said, 'We've been told not to talk to the media or the police.'

'*What?*'

'There was a memo. It said employees should not discuss company affairs with the media or the police, that every-thing will be dealt with by the management. Anyone who goes public without authorization is subject to summary dismissal.'

'Good God. They can't possibly hope to get away with forbidding you to talk to the *police!*'

'Toni, nobody wants to take things to a tribunal! Even if it ruled in your favour, you'd be branded as a troublemaker forever after, and nobody would touch you.' There was another silence, and then she said, 'About tomorrow evening . . .'

I'd almost forgotten my invitation to her. 'Yes?'

'I . . . don't know if I can make it.'

It stung, more sharply than I would have expected. 'What you mean is, you think it would be very bad for your career prospects if your new boss found out that you'd been to visit me.'

'It's not *my* fault!' Kath protested tearfully. 'I'd *like* to see you, but they're so angry. If I'm sacked everyone will think it was because I did something wrong, and if I quit, they'll give me a horrible reference, I just know they will. And I'm not *like* you, Toni, I can't just brush it off; I don't have a record people would notice, I'm just a PA, and when I'm nervous I go to pieces. I'd come over as pathetic in an interview. I'm sorry!'

'Yeah,' I snarled, 'me too.'

Mahogany
Swietenia macrophylla
South America

Listed as 'vulnerable' and on the CITES list
(Convention on International Trade in Endangered
Species of Wild Flora and Fauna) prohibiting
trade in threatened species

Six

I walked up and down the lounge a few times, too angry to sit still, then picked up the threatening letter and looked at it again. I took it over to the telephone and rang the police.

It was not a very satisfying telephone call. I provided the brusque receptionist with the incident number, and told her that I'd received threats and that I'd like to speak to whoever was responsible for the investigation. The receptionist told me that somebody would get back to me.

Two hours later, when nobody had, I went out to do some grocery shopping. My fridge was empty, and without my computer I couldn't use the delivery service.

I heard the phone ringing when I got back to the flat, but by the time I got the door open it had stopped. I didn't dial call-back: the walk home from the shops carrying heavy bags had brought on the headache. I took some co-codamol, bunged the chilled goods into the freezer, then lay down with a cold cloth over my eyes.

The phone rang again. I staggered over to it and picked it up with the cloth still held to my face.

'Antonia Lanchester?' A man's voice, unfamiliar. The police!

'Speaking.'

'This is Colin Douglas of Griffin Legal, acting on behalf of Masterpiece Home Design. I've been instructed to inform you that my clients intend to sue you for theft, breach of confidence and slander.'

Not the police. I pressed the cloth against the side of my face, feeling the socket of my right eye hollow against my palm. I was shocked, but somewhere underneath it, relieved. I now had a target for my sense of outrage. 'Have you *really*?'

There was a pause: this wasn't in his script. I set the cloth down and fumbled around the kitchen counter looking for a pen.

'This is not a trivial matter!' huffed the lawyer. 'My clients allege that you have stolen documents and acted maliciously in such a way as to severely damage their reputation. They intend to prosecute this forcefully!'

I dug my pen out of my handbag. 'What did you say your name was?'

After a wary, uncomfortable hesitation, he repeated it, along with the name of the legal firm and their phone number.

'And you're saying that Masterpiece Home Design are going to sue me?' I asked. '*Forcefully*? Can I have that in writing? For that matter, Mr Douglas, why are you phoning me in the first place? Isn't it more usual to send a letter? Or did you send the one I received earlier today?'

Another momentary pause. 'If you received a letter today, it wasn't from us. I'm phoning you because my clients still hope that the matter can be settled out of court.'

'Ah. So what do they want in exchange for withdrawing this threat?'

'I do not accept that description of their actions,' the lawyer replied instantly.

'They're not threatening to sue?'

'They are entitled to sue. They would prefer to settle out of court, given that you are, as I understand, in ill health.'

'Oh? So what you're saying is that they're worried I might snuff it before they get their pound of flesh?'

'They wish to spare you the stress of a court case, Ms Lanchester. They are willing to suspend their legal action if you cooperate with them in their efforts to clear their name.'

'Mr Douglas? Tell me this in writing, and I'll respond. Until then – fuck off.'

I cut off the call, then switched off the phone. I stood leaning against the counter, gripping the handset so hard it made my fingers hurt – until something made me look over at my new door.

A man stood there, watching me. He was young, dark-skinned, dressed in ragged jeans and a black T-shirt. He held a machete in his hand.

I caught my breath, then backed away into the lounge. I

was still holding the phone, and I held it up between me and the intruder. 'I'll phone the police!' I shrieked, and began pressing nines.

He took a step toward me, raising the machete, and I saw that the heavy blade was covered with blood. I put the headset to my mouth and screamed, 'Police! Help! Murder!' but the phone was dead against my ear. I remembered that I'd turned it off. Terrified, I looked back up – but the man with the machete was gone. Where he stood there were only trees, their trunks stretching away into green darkness. The headache crashed back down, blinding me.

Hallucination. I should have known – should have realized that the man came from my imagined Sarawak, and didn't belong in England. I stumbled over to the sofa and lay down.

It was about seven in the evening before I remembered that I'd left the phone switched off. When I switched it on again, it immediately started ringing.

'Ms Lanchester?' said a vaguely familiar male voice, not the lawyer's. 'Are you there?'

'Speaking.'

'Oh, good! Are you all right?'

I hesitated. 'Who is this, please?'

'Thomas Holden. From the Rainforest Trust. I've been trying to reach you for hours. We've had a . . . a . . . well, some trouble, and Nur Rashidah told me about what happened to you, so I thought we should meet and compare notes, but I couldn't get hold of you. Are you OK?'

'I had the phone off.'

'Oh, that's good. I mean, I'm glad nothing's happened to you.'

'You said you've had a break-in?'

'No, no! We've been *raided* by the police! Somebody told them we were a front for an Islamic terror organization, if you can believe it, and we had *fifteen* men come charging in first thing this morning! With *guns* and everything!' He laughed, as though this had been an exciting treat. 'They arrested me!'

'Good God. What—?'

'Lucky I'm not a Muslim! I'd still be there.'

'Nur Rashidah . . .'

'Oh, she had lectures this morning, luckily. It was just me in the office, and they let me go this afternoon – not that they apologized or anything. "I hope you understand that we must take all information of this nature very seriously" and so on. They've still got my computers, the one from the office and my own one from home. I can't do any work until I get them back. I can't even tell people what happened! God, we only have this office here because this sort of thing wasn't supposed to happen in England!'

'Oh my,' I said weakly.

'Anyway, I hope they'll come talk to you now, but even if they don't, I'd like to get together. Agree a common strategy or whatever.'

I felt distinctly feeble. 'Wait. You hope they'll come talk to me?'

'About Masterpiece Home Design. See, I told them about the files you gave us, and about the trouble you've been having. I said I thought their tip-off was just more of the same, the company trying to punish us, or maybe digging for dirt they could use against us. I don't know whether they believed me, but you'd expect them to check up on it. When could we get together? Would it be easier if we came to your place, or would you prefer Nur Rashidah to fetch you here?'

On the point of snapping 'Neither!' I checked myself: there was no reason to refuse. I meant, in some hazy way, to fight back. I could use allies.

It was possible, of course, that this police raid was nothing to do with the files I'd stolen. The Rainforest Trust undoubtedly had enemies in its Asian homelands: Nawaz had mentioned that its offices there were regularly shut down. Today's incursion might have been provoked by a more established enemy. On the other hand, the timing was suspicious, and the anonymous letter – still lying on my coffee table – showed that someone connected with MHD was willing to fight dirty.

'It's probably easier for me if you come here,' I told Thomas Holden. 'Would tomorrow after lunch suit?'

*   *   *

The police finally phoned back at nine the next morning. The officer I spoke to was not one of those who'd come to the flat; in fact, he didn't seem to know anything at all about my case, let alone Thomas Holden's. When I told him about the threatening note, he asked if I believed my neighbours were responsible. When I told him that I blamed my former employers, and why, he became openly sceptical. In the end, as a great concession, he agreed that someone could come round and take a statement. When? He couldn't say. I had to understand that the police were very busy on a Saturday.

'I need to go out this morning,' I told him, 'but I'll be in all afternoon and evening.'

Fine. Someone would come then.

My errand that morning was computer shopping: I needed to get back online quickly, not least to save myself the walk to the shops. I'd arranged for Nur Rashidah to fetch me at ten. She ferried me (slowly and cautiously, of course) over to a retail park where there was a computer superstore. When I'd bought a new machine, she loaded the boxes into the car, and, on our return to Canalside, insisted on carrying all of them upstairs to the flat herself. It took her three trips. 'Do you need some help to set them up?' she asked, when we had the array of cardboard cases lined up in the spare room.

'Are you good with computers?'

She hesitated, then shamefacedly shook her head. 'I know how to use one – but if it does not work, oh! I never know what to do. I look at what I've done, and I can never under-stand why it's wrong.'

'Yeah. Me too. Oh well, I suppose I can muddle through. I've managed before. Were you coming to this meeting this afternoon?'

She nodded seriously.

'Then why don't you stay for lunch?'

'I will cook something!' she agreed at once, smiling.

'I have some ready meals.'

'No, no, I will cook!'

However, it quickly emerged that she knew only a few recipes and that I did not have any of the ingredients she needed for those: no root ginger or lemongrass, no coconut milk, no peanut butter. Chagrined, she offered to go down to the shops. It was noon, however, so we agreed she could cook me a Malaysian meal another time. We ate a pasta ready meal, and Nur Rashidah longingly told me of the culinary delights of home. She was not, as I'd somehow assumed, from Sarawak, where her cousin had worked, but from cosmopolitan Kuala Lumpur. Her father was a government official, her mother a teacher; she had a younger sister and a brother. She missed her family very much, she admitted, and she found Britain cold and unfriendly. 'But the university has been very good,' she told me earnestly, embarrassed at criticizing my native country. 'The staff are most helpful, and I have been making friends.'

'I bet that at this time of year, though, you wish you were home.'

She smiled at that, and nodded. 'It is so dark here in the winter.'

I glanced at the grey sky that showed through the window. 'Yes. I miss the sun too. I want to get away for a bit, go somewhere warm.'

Thomas Holden, with Rafik Nawaz in tow, turned up while we were making coffee. He shook my hand warmly, but when he went into the lounge he stared for a moment at the bookcases and the occasional table, then gave me a reproachful look.

'The company gave me a discount,' I informed him wearily. 'If they offered it again, I wouldn't take it, but at the time I wasn't worried.'

Nawaz gave him an amused look. 'What, it's illegal hardwood?'

'That's *mahogany!*' exclaimed Holden, waving at the nearest bookcase. 'It's been on the CITES list for *years!*'

Nawaz grinned. 'So *that's* real mahogany! You know, it looks much better than stained pine!'

'Corporate flunky,' said Holden.

'Hippie,' replied Nawaz. The two men sat down and accepted coffees from Nur Rashidah.

'Were you two at school together?' I asked, curious to confirm it.

They both nodded. 'School *and* university,' supplied Nawaz.

'That's why I've come along to help him out.' He gave me a
grin. 'For what it's worth. In real life I'm a solicitor for the
city council. I advise them on planning applications. If this
turns into a court case, you're going to have to hire somebody
who knows what he's doing.'

'I doubt it'll go to court,' I told him, 'but I'll follow that
advice if it does.' I seated myself in the armchair, leaving
the sofa to the two men; Nur Rashidah, shy and silent, carried
in one of the chairs from the dining area and perched by the
breakfast bar.

'Tom told me you were burgled,' began Nawaz. 'He said
you think it had something to do with the documents you
gave the Rainforest Trust.'

'That's overstating it. It *could* have been a revenge attack
by my ex-boss, but it could also have been an ordinary
burglary.' I paused, thinking about it, then went on, 'I guess,
though, that I *do* think Ken was behind it. My PA, Kath
Stevens, phoned yesterday to ask if I knew where he was:
apparently the police have been asking for him, but he hasn't
been in to the office since Wednesday morning.'

Nawaz pursed his lips in a soundless whistle. 'Yah. Sounds
to me like he blew up, then went AWOL when he realized
he was going to get caught.'

I shrugged. 'I could be wrong. The police were investigating, but I don't know what they've found, or if they've
even found anything. I'm expecting someone to come round
this afternoon, incidentally: they may show up while you're
here. However, whether or not the burglary was Ken's work,
there's more that's happened since.'

They all sat up at that. 'Legal threats?' asked Nawaz.

'That too. I got a telephone call from MHD's lawyer – a
Colin Douglas at Griffin Legal. You know anything about them?'

Nawaz made a face. 'Griffin Legal's a high-powered city
firm. I've heard the name – I think they specialize in contract
law – but they're out of my league. I can ask around, if you
like.'

'I expect they're perfectly unexceptionable. Anyway, Mr
Douglas informed me that I'm going to be sued for slander
unless I cooperate with MHD's efforts to, quote, "clear their
name" unquote. I don't take it too seriously, Mr Nawaz . . .'

'Call me Rafi.'

'Rafi, then. It's never going to get to court in less than six months. Still, I think it shows that they're pretty stirred up. When Kath phoned, she also cancelled an engagement she'd made to come round for a drink – and it was perfectly clear that she did it because she was afraid she'd get in trouble for associating with me. She said that MHD is "in a flap", and that its employees have been instructed not to speak to the media – *or the police* – about any of this.'

Rafi's eyebrows went up.

'Then yesterday I received *this*.' I picked the threatening letter off the coffee table and opened it out so that everyone could read it. 'I phoned the police about it – it's one of the things I'm hoping to talk to them about if they show up. They don't seem very interested, though.'

Nur Rashidah, at my elbow, craned her neck to see, then flinched.

'That's *nasty*,' Thomas Holden commented, a bit breathlessly. He looked up at me, his long face worried.

I smiled back at him. 'Yes, and that's what makes it useful, if you follow me.'

He evidently did not: he frowned in bewilderment.

'I'm a PR director, Mr Holden – and a good one. I have contacts in the media, and this is a story they'll be willing to run. I asked the company lawyers to put their threat in writing, and I hope they comply. Combine an official threat with this note, and MHD's name will stink from shore to shore.'

'Wait a minute!' Rafi exclaimed. 'That nasty note may well be nothing to do with MHD's official response. It could just be your ex-boss again, or some other middle management type trying to scare you. You say they're already threatening to sue you for slander; if you make an accusation which turns out to be false, you'd just prove their case!'

I shook my head. 'Public opinion isn't a court of law: it's perfectly happy to convict on circumstantial evidence, or on hearsay, or on mere *suspicion*. I don't have to make any accusations, slanderous or otherwise. All I have to do is tell my story. Believe me, the public will be perfectly happy to join the dots.'

There was a silence.

'I think I would rather do this,' I told them all, slowly, feeling the shift of some internal balance as my mind made itself up. 'I would like to die with the sense that I've accomplished something. Thomas, when I said I could get this into the media, I meant I could get the *whole* story into the media – including the issue of illegal logging. I'll need your pictures of the Magoh River massacre, though. It won't really shock people unless they can see pictures. It was all too foreign and too far away.'

'We released pictures when it happened,' Thomas pointed out. 'Nobody paid any attention.'

'Yes, but now you have an *angle*. You have a story *here*, in Britain – and, if you don't mind my saying so, you have somebody who knows how to present it. People will pay attention now.'

They all stared at me.

'It would be great if you could do this,' Thomas said at last, a bit breathlessly. '*Great*. But my pictures of Magoh River were on my computer, and I don't know when I'll get it back.'

'Don't your associates in Malaysia have copies?'

'Yes, of course! But I . . . I don't even know if the police will let me use my internet connection. I suppose I could borrow, but I'd need something I can secure – I'm always on at our associates about keeping things secure; I can't suddenly tell them to upload stuff to some machine in an internet cafe!'

'You can use my computer,' I told him. 'Are you any good with them?'

'Yes,' he said, blinking. 'I mean, that's what my degree was in.'

'Oh, good! You can set it up then. It's brand new, bought this morning, and I haven't even switched it on yet. When you've got it working, maybe you could also get it to fetch my email.'

He was working on the computer when the police arrived, about an hour later. Rafi was advising me on how to avoid slander, while Nur Rashidah listened with a worried frown. When the doorbell rang, she was the one who got up to press

'We can use my story to draw attention to yours,' I went on. 'I agree with you, Mr Holden – all right, Thomas! I think there probably *is* a connection between the raid on your organization and the things that have happened to me. The public will think so, too. If you want to fight back, this is the way to go about it.'

'You think you can get this into the newspapers?' Thomas Holden asked uncertainly.

'Absolutely. Newspaper and local radio, easily; big news sites, probably. I'm not so sure about television, but I wouldn't rule it out.'

Nur Rashidah gave me a worried look. 'Mrs Lanchester, isn't this—'

'You can call me Toni. All my friends do.'

She replied with a sweet, shy smile, but went on seriously, 'Isn't this . . . too much for you to do? You are very ill. You said you wanted to go away, while you still could – to see the sun, you said, somewhere warm. Now you are talking about court cases and publicity campaigns. I don't . . . I don't think you could do both.'

It was something of a shock. I saw that I hadn't even *considered* how this would affect my plans for a holiday. And yet, she was right: it would be hard, if not impossible, to do both. My health had been getting worse since the diagnosis, and I didn't know how much longer I'd feel up to travelling. I wasn't even sure whether I'd be *allowed* to go, with a court case hanging over me.

You have only a few months left to live: do you spend it wrangling with the media over the phone, or lying on a beach in Barbados?

I didn't *know* anyone in Barbados, that was the rub. How much would I enjoy it, alone, sick with headaches, hallucinating? Could I even find an insurance company to cover me for the journey, or an airline willing to take me without insurance?

I'd wanted to escape the consequences of my theft, but I'd found out that, as the cynics say, no good deed goes unpunished. Perhaps it was for the best. The publicity campaign would certainly be more *interesting* than a beach in Barbados.

the intercom button, listen to the request, and admit the visitors to the building.

The men who eventually knocked on the door didn't look like police. There were two of them, both in their thirties, and they were in plain clothes – smart-casual trousers, dark jumpers worn over shirt and tie; one of them carried a briefcase. Their ID, however, which they showed me at the door, proclaimed them to be Detective Inspectors J. Summers and E. O'Connor. Summers was young, tall and saturnine; O'Connor was greying, fat and rumpled.

I couldn't believe that the sneerer at the police station had despatched two detective inspectors, and I wondered if this was the anti-terrorist squad. Thomas Holden, however, had come out of the study when they knocked, and he looked at the pair without recognition. If they had come to check out his story, they weren't the people who'd dealt with him before.

'What can I do for you?' I asked the men. 'Is this about my complaint?'

Both were taken aback. O'Connor smiled uncertainly. ''Fraid not. Mrs Lanchester, we're sorry to trouble you, but it would help us a lot if we could ask you some questions about Mr Kenneth Norman. Can we come in?'

This sounded ominous. I admitted them, however, and showed them into the lounge. They seated themselves on the sofa, side by side; O'Connor opened the briefcase and dug out a notebook and a pen. The Rainforest contingent hovered warily, and Detective Inspector Summers frowned at them. 'We need to conduct this interview in private, Mrs Lanchester.'

'If this has anything to do with my erstwhile employers, Masterpiece Home Design, then these people have an interest.'

Both detectives looked uncomfortable. 'Mrs Lanchester, it's standard procedure to conduct police interviews in private. For the security of our investigation, you understand.'

'We can go,' offered Thomas. 'Can I come back this evening, though? I still need to contact a load of people, tell them what happened, and, well, I've got your computer set up now.'

I told him he could come back that evening to use the computer, and he and the others filed out.

'Thank you,' Summers said when they'd gone. O'Connor did a preparatory scribble on his notepad, to check that the pen worked. It didn't. He blew out his cheeks and began to search in the briefcase; I got up, went over to the kitchen counter by the telephone, and fetched him one of my own pens. He gave me a grateful smile and began filling in the top of a page; it bore an array of slots under the bold-face title **Preliminary Interview** and the crest of the local CID. He looked up expectantly and asked me my full name, occupation, and date of birth.

'Oh, you're never that old!' he exclaimed when I told him the latter, attempting rogueish charm. Summers frowned at him.

When the formalities were over, they wanted to know about Ken – how well I knew him, what I thought of him. I told them. Had he ever visited me in the flat? I told them about his attempt the previous Saturday; it didn't seem to surprise them, and they were only concerned to establish that I hadn't let him in. I wondered, then, if they'd found his fingerprints on one of the CD cases, but I asked no questions. If Ken had been responsible for the break-in, the police could deal with him and welcome. I had other concerns.

We continued to my raid on Ken's computer and his reaction to it, and then to his phone calls and back to his abortive visit.

'Have you seen him since then?' asked Summers.

'No.' I hesitated. 'I did wonder if he was the one who broke into my flat last week. But that might have been just an ordinary burglar.'

They both looked up. 'We're aware, of course, of the break-in,' said Summers smoothly, giving nothing away. 'Could you tell us about it again, though? There could be something our colleagues missed.'

I told them about the burglary, perfunctorily at first, then, in response to their questions, at length. Yes, I was sure the intruder had gone into every room in the flat, there had been damage everywhere; yes, I was sure that my credit cards had been taken then, and not earlier or later; yes, I'd cancelled them pretty much as soon as I'd confirmed they were missing – it would've been about eleven on Wednesday. Nur Rashidah could confirm that. Yes, the computer was taken. Oh, it was an iMac, I didn't remember the model . . . Yes, I supposed I still had some of the instruction folders and disks, I could check . . .

'Yes, please,' said Summers.

I fetched the old computer bumpf from the heap of half-sorted junk in the study. Summers and O'Connor glanced through it, then exchanged a look of satisfaction. The police must have found the computer. In Ken's house, perhaps?

If they had, it hardly needed two detectives to convict him. Why were they so interested? Had Ken done a runner with company funds?

They didn't say, merely continued with their interrogation. No, I hadn't stayed in the flat after the burglary. I'd gone to a hotel – the Holiday Inn. No, of course I hadn't told Ken Norman I was going there! I supposed it had been about four in the afternoon when Nur Rashidah dropped me off there; she'd had a lecture to attend at two. I'd stayed until lunchtime on Friday. No, I hadn't left the hotel at all in between.

'Can you prove that?' asked Summers.

'I had a *brain biopsy* on Tuesday!' I told him indignantly. 'I would've thought it was *obvious* that I wasn't doing much gadding about!'

'We did hear about your illness,' said Summers soothingly. 'I'm very sorry.'

'Yeah,' put in O'Connor abruptly. He met my eyes, and surprised me with the real pity in his own. 'Horrible thing to happen to anyone, and a lovely woman like you – tragic. I'm sorry for you, truly I am.' I realized that the rogueish-ness earlier hadn't been a come-on, but a clumsy expression of the same pity, an attempt to cheer me up.

Summers frowned at him before turning back to me. 'It would be helpful if we could definitely establish your where-abouts between Wednesday and Friday.'

I stared. 'What *is* this?'

The two men looked at one another, and then Summers said slowly, 'Mr Norman's body was discovered this morning.

It has been suggested that you may have been connected to his death.'

I kept staring, unable to take it in. 'Ken's *dead*?' I asked stupidly. Then, finally understanding what he meant, 'You think *I* killed him?'

'Mrs Lanchester, at this stage we're just trying to build up a picture of Mr Norman's movements. He told several people that he intended to speak to you. Would the hotel staff know if he'd tried to contact you? And would they be able to testify as to your whereabouts?'

I swallowed, suddenly feeling very sick. *His body was discovered this morning.* Where? How had he died?

I imagined Ken hauled out of the canal – swollen and glassy-eyed, his ridiculous too-tight trousers still gaping on his sodden underwear. I squeezed my eyes shut. My head began to throb.

It has been suggested that you may have been connected . . .

Who'd suggested that?

Do you know what you've done? You have to fucking die, so you're going to take me with you, is that it?

'Mrs Lanchester?'

'Please,' I choked. 'Let me . . . I'm not well, please leave me alone a minute.'

There was silence for a couple of minutes. I sat bent over, pressing my hands against my eyes and trying to breathe slowly and evenly, praying that I wouldn't start seeing things. It seemed to work: the throbbing faded, and at last I felt it was safe to sit up and open my eyes. The detectives' faces watched me from behind the red-rimmed blotches my hands' pressure had left on my retinas, Summers' guarded, O'Connor's again full of pity.

'Would the staff at the Holiday Inn be able to testify as to your whereabouts?' Summers asked again.

'I . . . I suppose so. I checked in and checked out, and I used room service a lot. But I didn't . . . That is, I can't *prove* that I never left the room.' I thought a moment, then added, 'I didn't have my car – I'm not supposed to drive any more. Nur Rashidah, my driver, dropped me off and then parked the car . . . I don't even know if she left it here or if she took it back to her own place. You could check with her, though, couldn't you? And you could check that I didn't take any taxis?'

'We could. That's helpful. Did the hotel staff ever say that someone was trying to contact you while you were there?'

'No.'

'Not even your driver?'

'She called me on my mobile.'

'Could we study your mobile then, to check for missed calls? I'm sorry to inconvenience you, but it would be incredibly useful if we could, say, determine that Mr Norman tried to phone you at some particular time.'

'He didn't. He couldn't. I told you, I'd blocked his calls.'

'He might have called on a friend's phone, or from a phone box. Even if he didn't, it would be useful if we could rule it out. Mrs Lanchester, it's in your own interest for you to establish where you were and what you were doing.'

Wordlessly, I dug my mobile out of my bag and handed it to Detective Summers. O'Connor at once dug a bag out of the briefcase to hold it. He wrote out a label for it, then wrote me a receipt, which both men signed.

'We'll get that back to you as soon as we can,' he told me with a smile.

'We would also appreciate it,' said Summers, 'if you gave your doctor permission to discuss your case with us.'

'What? Why?'

'Your illness is clearly a factor that has to be considered,' Summers said blandly.

O'Connor, however, volunteered an unedited version. 'We've been told you're suffering from delusions. Now, I don't think you are, but what I think's no matter to anyone. We need to get an expert opinion on it.'

I stared again, speechless, and he raised a hand defensively. 'I don't believe it; told you that already, didn't I? Only if we get expert testimony on it right away it saves us trouble.'

I set my teeth, suddenly understanding how MHD intended to defend itself. *Poor Antonia! Her brain is badly affected; she doesn't know what she's saying.* 'Did the people who told you I was delusional tell you what it was that I took from Ken's computer?'

They both hesitated. 'Something to do with the company selling furniture made from illegally logged timber, wasn't it?' O'Connor ventured uncertainly.

I took them both into the study, where the computer was still switched on. Thomas had by then obtained his copies of the Magoh River pictures, and I selected them and set the machine to display them as a slideshow.

'The result of an illegal logging operation,' I told the police, and they recoiled.

The Malaysian Rainforest associates had also sent Thomas duplicates of the incriminating letters. I quit the photos and opened the letter files. 'MHD knew that one of its sister companies was probably involved in that massacre,' I told the two detectives. 'They provided them with financial support to help them "clear themselves" – see?' I stood back to let the police study the letters. '*That's* what I gave the Southeast Asian Rainforest Trust, and I *know* my erstwhile employers are very angry about it, because a friend there told me as much. She also told me that staff have been instructed not to discuss any of this with the police.'

'"Evidence of connection between our company and the perpetrators of this atrocity would be extremely damaging to us."' O'Connor read out thoughtfully. 'Who's Howard?'

'*Howarth*. MHD's director, Alfred Howarth.'

'So – right at the top of the company, then. Not an underling.'

I nodded. 'Since I handed those letters to the Rainforest Trust, my flat's been broken into, I've been threatened with legal action by MHD, and I've received an anonymous note threatening to make my last months hell on earth. The Rainforest Trust, in the meantime, has been closed down because of some kind of tip-off that it's a front for an Islamic terrorist organization – which it clearly is *not*. What conclusions you draw from all that is up to you, of course. All I insist on is that these things are *events*, not delusions.'

Summers looked at me with misgiving. O'Connor, however, frowned and asked, 'What's this about a threatening note?'

Both the detectives took a gratifying interest in the threatening note. They wanted to take it with them, to study; they extracted a folder from the briefcase and enclosed the tatty sheet of paper carefully within it, then labelled and dated it. I was obliged to write out a statement concerning the item: when I had received it, where I had opened it and so on. Summers phoned the local police station to discover what had happened to the regular enquiry.

I hoped to overhear a reprimand, but the discussion was moderate and polite. It seemed that the local police had, in fact, assigned someone to visit me about the threat; that he hadn't yet made it was due to the pressure of 'more urgent' matters. The detectives informed the local station that they had discussed the situation with me, and that they would drop off a report.

'I'd suggest, though,' Summers went on, 'that if Mrs Lanchester reports any other problems, you prioritize your response. Understand, my colleague and I are investigating a *homicide* possibly connected to this. Any threat she receives should be taken very seriously.'

I didn't hear the response to that, obviously, but O'Connor, not satisfied with it, gave me his own mobile number before he left.

Teak
Tectona grandis
India and Southeast Asia

Cultivated in plantations

Seven

When the two detectives had left I once again prowled restlessly up and down the lounge, too disturbed to sit still. Ken was dead? *Murdered?*

Did they actually suspect *me*? Summers had dodged the question when I asked it. Or maybe not; maybe at this stage the police really *were* just trying to trace Ken's movements, and didn't suspect anybody. It made sense that they had to evaluate the situation before they decided who merited further investigation.

I wondered how he'd died; again my imagination presented me with his body being dragged from the canal. That, though, was pure fantasy: nobody had said anything about what killed him.

I went back to the computer, which was still switched on, and typed 'Ken Norman' into Google. I got a couple of hits on men in Pasadena or Iowa, then some of my own PR releases for MHD. I tried the name of the local paper, and discovered that it didn't have a website. If I wanted to read the story, I'd have to walk down to the shops . . . where I'd find that the news had yet to be released. *Mr Norman's body was discovered this morning* . . . No, there'd be nothing in the paper, not yet.

Do you know what you've done? You have to fucking die, so you're going to take me with you, is that it?

What had he meant by that?

I remembered him shouting at me through the intercom: *I need to know . . . Please, just tell me . . .*

Tell him what? What I'd taken? Where I'd taken it? Surely he knew!

The phone rang, making me jump. I picked it up gingerly.

'Mrs Antonia Lanchester?' A deep male voice, entirely unfamiliar.

My heart began a slow, sick pounding. 'Speaking.'

'I'm Robert Tower of the CID; I'm calling in connection with an investigation into an alleged terrorist organization . . .'

Thomas Holden's anti-terrorist squad! Dizzy with relief, I sat down – then wondered why I'd been so afraid. Who had I *thought* that deep voice belonged to?

The anti-terrorist unit wanted confirmation of what Thomas had told them. I confirmed it, and referred them to Summers and O'Connor as well as to my original report of the burglary. At this Robert Tower said they would have to interview me. He asked me to come down to the central police station.

'What, *now*?' I asked, startled: it was by this time nearly five o'clock on a Saturday evening.

Detective Tower grudgingly allowed that I did not have to rush out the door, and made me an appointment for the following Monday.

I set the phone down, then stared blankly at the teak of the breakfast bar. The wood was marked with a ring from somebody's coffee cup. I went into the kitchen, dampened a dishcloth, and wiped the offending mark away.

The cloth came away red. I stared at it for a moment, then turned appalled eyes back to the teak counter. It was now covered in snow, spattered redly with thick gouts of blood.

I shut my eyes, dropped the dishcloth, and stood still, trying to control my breathing. It was another hallucination, nothing more. I felt my way back around the breakfast bar to the sofa and sat down.

Silence. The hum of the refrigerator; the gurgle of a drainpipe; the noise of the wind against the window, of a car passing in the street below. I opened my eyes again: no snow, no blood. The dark wood of the counter gleamed moistly where I'd wiped it, marked by nothing more than water.

Ken *was* dead, though. Summers and O'Connor had been no hallucination.

Had I told them that Ken had accused me of taking him with me into death? Had I said that he'd turned up asking me – no, *begging* me – to tell him . . .

Tell him what? I'd never even allowed him to say what it was. I'd sent him off, so preoccupied with my own wounds that I'd barely noticed how odd it was for him to be asking me to *tell* him anything.

He'd tried to bribe me, too, to 'discuss the situation' with him. Had I told the detectives that?

I couldn't remember. I went back to the phone, found O'Connor's number, and dialled it.

He answered promptly, listened to my awkward supplement without comment, then thanked me. 'You did mention some of that before,' he added, 'but it's good to have the whole picture.'

'I don't know what it was he wanted to discuss,' I admitted. The shame of that suddenly hit, hot and salty. I hadn't been willing to listen to him, and now he was dead. 'I'm sorry!'

'It may not have been anything,' O'Connor replied soothingly. 'He may have told himself he wanted to know why you did it, when really he just wanted an excuse to shout at you. It would've been a big mistake for you to let him in, I'm sure of that.'

I was not so sure.

Thomas turned up a little while later to use the computer. I told him about Ken, not because I expected him to do anything, but because it made me feel better to tell someone.

'Wow!' he said, frightened and impressed. Then he looked away, embarrassed by the childish exclamation. 'That is . . . I, uh, I'm sorry. That's . . .'

'I was shocked,' I told him, when he didn't seem to know what adjective to use.

'Yeah. It's shocking.'

'He wanted to talk to me, but I don't know *why*!'

'Revenge.' Thomas waved a hand at the stacks of CDs still waiting to be shelved. 'I mean, the stuff came off *his* computer, and the company was blaming him. He was furious with you.'

Again, it didn't satisfy me. Yes, Ken had been furious; yes, I did suspect that he was responsible for trashing my flat – but he *had* wanted to talk to me. 'It still doesn't make sense. He obviously *knew* what I'd done, because it had come back to bite him – so why was he asking me about it?'

Thomas shrugged. 'Maybe he didn't know how *much* you'd

got. I mean, *I* don't know exactly how much you got. You
gave us two letters and a spreadsheet, but I've been assuming
you cherry-picked those. There must've been more than that
on the disk. Do you still have it?'

I stared stupidly. I was a PR director with a degree in
English Literature; I thought of information in terms of documents. It had never occurred to me that I could simply have
copied everything on Ken's hard drive and gone through it
at my leisure.

'I didn't put anything on a disk!' I blurted, ashamed now
that I hadn't. 'I just went through his computer, and printed
out the things which I thought would be useful.'

'Oh!' He was surprised. 'Oh, *right*. Well, maybe that's
what he wanted to know: how much stuff you actually got.'

I thought about this. Could there have been *worse* on the
computer than the documents I'd stolen?

It didn't seem likely that MHD had known more, condoned
more, than what I'd seen. There could, though, have been
things which weren't *worse* so much as *different*, implicating
other people or other companies. Ken might have wanted to
offer the management some estimate of what they needed to
protect.

Surely, though, the company already *knew* where it was
being attacked?

'It'd make sense,' Thomas went on, warming to the idea.
'I mean, he *searched* this place, didn't he? And he took your
computer. And getting our offices raided – that meant *we*
couldn't use our computers and get out any more information than we had already!'

'But why would they think you were holding any information in reserve? You're just a . . . a coordinator for the
different environmentalist groups in Malaysia and Indonesia,
isn't that right? Anyone who knew about you would *presume*
you'd already sent everything I gave you to a dozen different
destinations – wouldn't they?'

Thomas deflated slightly. 'Maybe they just wanted to make
it harder for us to organize.' He frowned. 'What happened
with the anti-terrorism unit, anyway? Did they ever contact
you?'

I told him about Detective Tower's phone call.

'Stupid,' he said, shaking his head. 'All those guys working through the weekend. You think about it, it must be costing *thousands* of pounds in salaries and overtime. You'd think they'd want to make some kind of preliminary assessment before they committed themselves to an investigation, just so they wouldn't burn up their whole budget on false alarms.'

'It must have looked credible, on the face of it,' I pointed out. 'I mean, you *are* a western front for a group of organizations based in Muslim countries, many of which *have* been periodically shut down by the authorities . . .'

'Yeah, but you'd think the police could tell the difference between mullahs and orangutans!'

'I don't know – they're both pretty hairy.'

He laughed and went to work on my new computer. I made us both coffee, then sat and read for a bit. It was comforting to have him in the next room, shuffling the chair about and occasionally exclaiming. I hated that I felt that way – when I'd first got the flat, I'd revelled in the liberty and peace of *being on my own*, free from the dead weight of Ian. It seemed a humiliating lapse into dependence that I should be glad of the presence of a man – even of a young semi-stranger who was only interested in my computer. I was sorry, though, when he went home.

'I set up your email for you,' he told me as he left. 'I didn't look at it, but there's a lot. I think maybe you need a better spam filter. Let me know if you do; there's a really good free one on this geek site I know. I could install it for you.'

What was choking my inbox, however, wasn't just spam. When I opened Outlook the following morning, the message headings popped out one after another: *Super-Big Dick! Massive Cock! Suck Me, Baby!*

I recoiled, staring; the message headings continued to burst into my inbox, a catalogue of obscene invitations. Many of them had attachments which, judging from their size, must be photos.

I started to delete – click, click, click – but more of the things simply flowed up the screen in place of the ones I'd excised. Click, click, click . . . Then I realized I'd just deleted a message from a friend. I opened the 'Deleted Items' folder and retrieved it. *Dear Toni, I am so shocked and sorry at your news I can't think straight. I don't know what to say . . .*

Above her helpless grief, the neighbouring message heading proclaimed *Massive Stiffy!*

I quit the program, shaking. I'd been spammed by porn sites before – who hasn't? – but this intrusion was another order of magnitude.

It wasn't hard to guess that the person who'd sent me the note had posted my details on a chatroom or website, as a taste of how he could make my life 'hell on earth'. I could guess he was one of those misogynists who uses sex to dehumanize women so that he wouldn't have to deal with them as people. I wondered if it was Ken who'd done this: I could believe that of him. It seemed of a piece with that aborted credit-card purchase of a 'lovebed' – which, it had emerged, had been ordered from an internet retailer, to be delivered to my address at Canalside. That purchase had clearly been intended to harrass and humiliate *me*, not to gratify the purchaser, and this seemed to be more of the same.

If it had been Ken, there would clearly be no more of it. I needed to find the site, remove the details. I needed to sort through that heap of obscene emails – I'd lost many of my friends' email addresses when my computer was stolen, and I needed to get them back. I should simply delete all the filth and put the senders on the blocked list, then save the messages from my friends.

I couldn't do it; couldn't bring my wounded brain to confront that torrent of graphic obscenity. I sat at my desk, staring at the screen, unable to summon up my own email program in the safety of my own home. I told myself it was absurd. I was a confident, successful career woman, not a timid virgin: why should I find this flood intimidating? It wasn't even intended as harrassment, not by the senders. They presumably thought I'd invited it; probably most of them would be horrified if they knew the truth.

I still couldn't face it. There was something so horrible about the juxtaposition of condolences and e-porn that I was sickened; I felt that if I had to wade through it I would vomit.

My desktop photo disappeared; the screensaver came on, a tranquil image of falling water. I continued to sit there, staring at it numbly.

Leaf-shadows dappled the waterfall. I looked up, then turned, swivelling the desk chair. The rainforest had appeared at the study wall, and in the shadowy doorway the murdered boy stood, his little face anxious. I smiled weakly. He smiled back, his face lighting up, then moved silently forward on bare feet, once again holding out his hand.

The phone rang. I blinked, and the boy was gone, taking the forest with him: only the bare walls were left, and the water falling endlessly across the screen. The phone rang again.

I stumbled into the lounge, dizzy. It took me another four rings to find the phone; when I finally answered it, it turned out to be my mother.

I'd phoned her from the hotel and told her the results of the biopsy; she'd been speechless with horror and grief, and I'd cut off before she could find anything to say. Now she was phoning to tell me that I should come home.

'You shouldn't have to manage on your own!' she told me. 'You need someone to . . . to *look after* you, to fetch and carry and cook and do the laundry, to be there, to take care of you! I've started clearing out your old room; I could have it ready for you tomorrow.'

I was seriously tempted. I *wanted* to be taken care of; if it came right down to it, I wanted to be mothered. Even the thought of her perpetually gabbling television, her taste for imbecilic Australian soaps and gruesome reality shows couldn't overpower that desire; even the memory of our frequent quarrels couldn't dull it. I wanted to be *safe*, away from burglaries and murderers and libidinous emails; I wanted to hide away, and die in peace.

To go home *tomorrow*, though, just when I'd intended to start my publicity campaign – I couldn't. It would be running away from the battle without firing a single shot; it would be letting the bastards get away with it. I couldn't.

'Thanks very much, Mum,' I said, choking on the words. 'I *will* come home. But not just yet. I've just committed to doing some PR for a charity, and I need to finish that first.

Besides,' I added as a cast-iron excuse, 'I need to sort out
the flat. You don't want to have to clear it, I know that.'

She conceded that she did not, but surprised me by volun-
teering to help. 'I can come up there this week,' she offered.
'I don't mind helping; it's just having to decide what to do
with everything that I can't manage.'

I hesitated, deeply touched. Then reality bit: my mother's
'help' would make the task more difficult. She was a packrat,
always had been: she could never bear to throw anything
out. Her attic overflowed with dusty curtains and old magazines; she had once driven two hundred miles to deliver an
old sideboard to a cousin who could've bought one locally
for less than the cost of the petrol. If she assisted me, we'd
end up shipping all the furniture to her brother's family in
Montreal – if we didn't quarrel over it and end up not
speaking to one another.

Actually, I supposed, the chances of her not speaking to
her dying daughter were nil – but still, it seemed better to
avoid a source of friction.

'That's very sweet,' I told her, 'but I don't think it would
work, Mum. I'm going to *throw things out.*'

She gave a sigh of acknowledgement.

'I will come home,' I assured her. 'When I've finished
here. When I know when that will be, I'll tell you, OK?'

'OK,' she said resignedly. 'But . . . do come home, please.
I want time with you while we still have some.'

My eyes stung. 'Yes. Yes, I'll come home.'

I cried after the phone call, but, oddly felt much better. I
took some co-codamol, went back to the study, and stared
at the screensaver.

I couldn't face the email, but there was no real reason why
I *should.* Thomas was planning to use my computer until he
had his own back, and he'd undoubtedly be willing to deal
with the inbox, then install something to filter for sexual
content to ensure that I didn't get any more unwanted solic-
itations. I ought to phone him – and the police. I wasn't sure
what crime it was, to post somebody's email address on a
porn site without their knowledge – but I *was* sure it couldn't
be legal.

*   *   *

The detectives' advice to the local police had had an effect after all: an officer arrived at the flat that same afternoon, despite the fact that it was still the weekend.

Thomas was there when he arrived, installing his spam filter. The obscene emails had all gone into the 'deleted items' folder, but only after he'd saved them on to a disk, which he presented to the policeman. He'd also identified the website that had inspired my correspondents, a charming place called cocksucker.com – he'd found it by the simple expedient of opening the emails until he found one that referred back to it. He accessed it for us and showed me the entry.

The photo was a familiar one: me smiling and professional in a dark jacket and green scarf. The text, however, was quite different. *Hi! I'm Toni, and I just love big dicks . . .* It degenerated from there.

'I can send a message to the site, telling them to take it off at once,' Thomas told me and the policeman, 'but I thought you should see it first.'

The policeman turned to me. 'And you had nothing to do with this?'

'How can you ask her that?' demanded Thomas, suddenly furious. 'Why would she have called you, if she'd *asked* for this? You know she's received threats, because she blew the whistle on her employers – didn't anybody mention that? You know she's dying of brain cancer – and some scum knew that, and did this anyway!'

'I had nothing to do with it,' I said into the silence. 'The picture is the one I use on my CV: anyone at the company would have had access to it. My credit card, which was stolen on Tuesday while I was in hospital, was used on Tuesday night to order a sex toy. I have no doubt that this was intended as harrassment. It may have been my ex-boss who was responsible, but that's just a suspicion.'

'What's your boss's name and address, then?' asked the policeman, taking out a notebook.

'Kenneth Norman – but he's dead. They told you to prioritize any complaint of mine because it was connected to a homicide, didn't they? He's the one who died. The detectives investigating it are called O'Connor and Summers. You should probably talk to them.'

The policeman, subdued, accepted Thomas's disk of offensive emails – plus a download of the entry – to preserve as evidence. He gave me an incident number and authorization to threaten the website with the law if they didn't remove the entry immediately.

'Thank you,' I told Thomas, when the policeman had gone again.

He shrugged. 'I'm just sorry we got you into this.'

I stared at him. 'Excuse me? I got *you* into this!'

'Well . . . but . . . we signed up for this – at least, I did. I've been trying to save the planet since I was in primary school. You . . . well, you found out you were ill and . . . and—'

'Made a bad decision on impulse?' I finished sourly.

'Not a *bad* decision,' he conceded. 'But . . . I don't know, I just feel we took advantage of you. You were reeling from a huge blow, and you hadn't taken time to think things through.' He looked down guiltily and added, 'That thing Nur Rashidah said, that you'd wanted to get away somewhere warm, to see the sun before . . . to sit in the sun one more time – I keep thinking of that. I'm sorry. You're not going to get the chance to do that, are you? And it's our fault.'

'Thomas.'

He looked up again, eyes very blue, very sad. My feelings wobbled for a moment – I have a weakness for blue eyes – but he was much too young for me, even if I hadn't been bound for the grave.

'I don't regret what I did,' I told him. 'I regret ever working for Masterpiece Home Design – but I don't regret giving you those files.'

'You're a hero,' he told me fervently.

I wasn't. I'd converted to trying to save the planet only because I could no longer profit from exploiting it. Still, it was nice that Thomas thought so.

Monday morning's post brought a couple more get-well cards; it also brought the official threat from Griffin Legal. The letter said very much what Colin Douglas had said over the phone. Masterpiece Home Design were preparing to take legal action in respect of my theft of company property and breach of confidence – but, in view of my illness, were willing to drop the charges if I assisted them in 'clearing their name'. I studied the document carefully, and found it satisfactory. It might conform to every law in the land, but it was unmistakeably still a threat. I could use it.

I'd been waiting until after the weekend to start my publicity campaign: there was no sense antagonizing journalists by contacting them out of hours at home. I had done some preparation, though, and now I was able to get straight to work. I phoned my five most influential contacts and explained the situation, then emailed them a press release.

I'd drafted the release on Sunday afternoon. It had been an extremely difficult document to draw up, not so much because of the need to avoid libel as because it was hard to decide how much of myself to reveal. My instinct was to stand back, to use the third person and give a purely objective account of MHD's misdeeds. I knew, however, that the more personal I made my statement, the more attention it would get – and the most dramatic and attention-grabbing element of all was my cancer. 'Whistleblower Accuses Employer of Harrassment' would get a couple of column inches on the business page. 'Company Harrasses Dying Woman' would get two columns and a photograph in UK news.

The trouble was, I didn't want to display my bloody wounds in public. I've always despised the modern appetite for the public confessional. I hate freak-show television; the taste for it always seems to me vampirish and voyeuristic. Despite that, I'd used some of the techniques in my PR work, for the simple reason that the personal story connects and grabs attention like nothing else. It had never before been my *own* story that I put in the spotlight, though. I wasn't willing to weep to camera – but it would be stupid not to play my strongest card.

In the end, I compromised. The statement I produced was personal but cool, dignified, even a bit sarcastic: one I could live with. I added names at the hospital and the police, so that sceptical editors could verify the story, and included Thomas's name and mobile number as a further source. I

attached my CV photo, along with the text of the legal letter
and the threatening note. I said nothing libellous. I admitted
freely that the note was anonymous – as I'd told Thomas,
the public would join the dots. When I sent the little package
off I felt as elated as I had when I first delivered my stolen
evidence to the Rainforest Trust. Whatever happened next,
I hadn't gone without a fight.

Nur Rashidah arrived after lunch, to transport me to the
police station for my interview with the anti-terrorism squad.
This turned out to be a non-event: the investigation had by
now concluded that the tip-off had been false. When I arrived,
I was obliged to wait for half an hour while the receptionist
tried to find out who was supposed to interview me; in the
end word came back that nobody was. The investigation was
being abandoned, and I wasn't needed after all. I could go
home.

Home I went. Back at my own computer, I drafted a blis-
tering letter to Robert Tower, suggesting that the police should
at least take an interest in who had wasted so much of their
time and resources with a false and malicious tip-off. Posting
it gave me another surge of satisfaction. It probably says
something shameful about me that self-righteous anger made
me feel better – but it did. It lifted my spirits no end.

I felt even better next day when I looked at the newspapers.

Nur Rashidah and Thomas brought them round that
morning. There was a thick stack. My story was in all the
titles I'd contacted. It wasn't the front page, of course, but
it was quite reasonably prominent, and my CV photo smiled
above quite large chunks of my carefully crafted text. Illegal
logging and the Magoh River massacre were mentioned,
too – tangentially, it was true, but they were there. 'Ms
Lanchester leaked documents revealing the company's links
to a dispute over illegal logging in Malaysia in which forty-
one protesters were killed.'

'Do you think the press will follow it up?' Thomas asked
anxiously.

In one of those too-pat coincidences, his phone rang
before I could answer: the press were indeed prepared to
follow it up.

My phone soon started ringing as well, and by the end of the afternoon I'd agreed to four interviews: two for national dailies, one for a Sunday supplement, one – to my great satisfaction – for the regional television news. Thomas had left by that stage, eyes bright with excitement, to do an interview of his own.

I was sitting on the sofa, relaxing after the excitement with a cup of cocoa, when the phone rang again. I picked it up.

'Toni?' asked a voice from the past.

It was like a jolt of electricity, like a sudden touch of ice to the back of the neck. I had forgotten all about him – or rather, hadn't made the connection that he would finally learn what I'd been unable to tell him.

'Ian.'

'In the paper,' he said breathlessly. 'I . . . I opened it up, and there you were. It said you were dying.'

'I tried to write you,' I told him defensively. 'I tried twice. The letters just came out wrong.'

'It's true, then?'

'What? Do you think I'd *lie* about something like that?'

'I . . . No, of course not! I'm just shocked, Toni. Stunned.'

'I did try to write you,' I repeated, pointlessly.

'Oh, God. It said you had brain cancer?'

'Something called an astrocytoma. The neurologist gave me two to six months.'

Even as I said it, the nasty realization dawned: that had been nearly three weeks ago. My time, my precious time, was flowing away.

Stand still, you ever-moving spheres of heaven,
that time may cease and midnight never come!
. . . the stars move still, time runs, the clock will strike,
the devil will come, and Faustus must be damned.

'They can't operate?'

'They said not.'

'I'm so sorry!'

There was a silence, and then Ian said, 'The story in the paper. It said that the company you worked for has been threatening you. Can I help?'

All the feelings lying dormant since our marriage foundered boiled up into the back of my throat: anger, frustration, bitterness, and, underneath them, making them all worse, love. 'Bit *late* for that, isn't it?'

'If you'd *told* me . . .'

'I don't mean *now*! I mean it's a bit late for *you* to be offering to *help*!'

'Oh, don't start this again! Just because I didn't do my share of the house cleaning!'

'Because you were a *dead weight*, Ian; because I was doing all the work, physically *and* emotionally, and I was trying to hold down a job at the same time, and it was too much. And I *asked* you to help, again and again, and you just didn't think it was important! You just sat around, all day, playing those damned computer games and waiting for the perfect role to turn up! And then, if you got a good role, oh, then you were out all hours, leaving me to sit at home; you'd say you needed to unwind after the show, but you never wanted to do anything with *me,* to give *me* a chance to unwind as well; you preferred—'

'I'm *sorry*! I said I was sorry before . . .'

'No, you didn't! You said I was being ridiculous!'

'Toni, Toni, please! I didn't phone you to start this again!'

Another silence, this one hot; I could hear my own quick, angry breathing.

'I'm sorry,' Ian said rapidly. 'I'm sorry I didn't help. I'm sorry that this terrible thing has happened to you. I . . . I'm still angry, too, if it comes to that, OK? I *loved* you, I couldn't see why . . . But no, let's just *stop*, OK? Please? I can't stand the thought that you're going to die still angry with me. I need to see you again, to make peace. And I'd like to help, if I can. I really *want* to help now. Please, please, don't let's just quarrel.'

My eyes stung. 'I don't want to,' I told him, blurting it out, the messy, hopeless truth. 'That was why I couldn't write you.'

'Please let me come and help. There must be things I could do.'

There had once been so many things I wanted him to do. I'd wanted him to love me, to be a real partner; I'd wanted a solid marriage, a sharing of lives in sickness and in health. I'd wanted us to have children and grow old together – and all my wants had been in vain. Now the black hole inside my skull would suck me in, whatever I wanted. It was time to put bitterness behind me.

Odd that I had to put aside the past, when I had so little future left.

'OK,' I said at last. 'I'd like to see you again. To say goodbye.'

We agreed that he would drive up from London on Friday evening.

My mother, my brother, and several friends also telephoned over the next couple of days. They, too, had seen the news, and were outraged to learn that Masterpiece Home Design was persecuting me. 'Why didn't you tell me?' my mother demanded angrily, and I muttered shamefaced excuses about not wanting her to worry, while acknowledging to myself that I hadn't wanted her to interfere.

The company itself produced a statement denying all responsibility for the harrassment. (They discreetly ignored the threatened lawsuit.) Instead, they suggested – as I'd expected – that I was delusional. They went so far as to imply that I'd faked the harrassment – though, of course, their new PR firm was canny enough to cloak this in pity for the dreadful illness which was making me confuse reality with sick imaginings. A British furniture retailer, they pointed out, couldn't possibly be held responsible for what a Chinese timber supplier did in Malaysia.

'Ms Lanchester was a valued employee of Masterpiece Home Design for three years,' they said, 'and it particularly saddens us that her illness has isolated her from her friends.'

The story, however, was big enough that the media which carried MHD's statement contacted me at once for my response – something I was grateful for, since if I'd responded the following day I would have been relegated to a note on an inner page and ignored. I was lucky in that I was able to prove that I couldn't have faked the harrass-ment. The burglary had occurred while I was in hospital, and it had emerged that my details had been sent to the porn site on Tuesday evening, from my own computer – which had of course been stolen in the burglary. It wasn't enough to quell the allegations of paranoia completely; once something like that's been raised, it hangs in the air for a long time, regardless of evidence. It did make MHD look dodgy, though.

I didn't have to say anything about the Malaysian connection: Thomas did that. The media were finally taking an interest in the massacre, and he was making the most of it. To tell the truth, he was making *too much* of it for really effective PR. He tried to pack too many details into each interview. The journalists had trouble following him, or got bored, and most of what he said came out garbled. The incriminating letters, however, generally emerged intact.

It was enough to get the issue into the public eye at long last. One of the national dailies produced a two-page spread about illegal logging, and another ran a 'How to Ensure that *Your* Furniture is Green!' article in a box under the Forestry Stewardship Council tree-and-checkmark logo.

Thomas was elated; I was merely pleased. The publicity would die down, and when it did, MHD and its ilk would still be selling tropical hardwoods. Still, the incident would have had an effect – there would be a big dent in the market. Even people who considered the fuss over the top would think twice about buying mahogany, as *other* people might, perhaps, look down on them because of it.

The decline in popularity of tropical hardwoods was a slow, incremental change, but it had been underway well before the Magoh River incident. My stolen documents and publicity campaign would contribute to that change – the latest wave of a green tide that was slowly rising on the consumerist shores of the West. At some point Western furniture retailers would decide that selling uncertified mahogany, ebony, teak or rosewood was simply not worth it. Better to go with certified timber: that's where the market growth was.

Probably it wasn't enough to save the rainforests, not with China and the rest of the developing world still happy to chop them down, not with the market for palm oil expanding and the plantations that supplied it steadily encroaching on the preserves. Much more was needed – trade agreements, tariffs, international legislation – but still, it was something. I would not have to go empty-handed to the grave.

Oak
Quercus robur
Europe

Abundant

Eight

Ken's death had made the local paper on Monday, but only as a brief notice taken from the police report. It seemed that his body had been found on Saturday morning by his ex-wife and his daughter when they arrived at his house to drop the daughter off for a weekend with her father. The police, said the report, were making inquiries.

I'd been vaguely aware that Ken was divorced, but I hadn't known that he had a daughter: he'd never spoken of her. It was disconcerting and depressing to think of this girl arriving to spend a weekend with her father and making such a ghastly discovery. How old was she? Had she *enjoyed* spending week-ends with him? What was she feeling now?

All these were questions I could neither ask nor answer. Caught up in my own press campaign, I tried to avoid thinking about Ken at all. When he crossed my mind – as happened more frequently than I would have liked – I shied away, forcing myself instead to plan my next interview, or read the newspaper.

I was not allowed to ignore the matter completely, however. On Tuesday – the day my campaign hit the papers – I received a phone call from Detective Inspector O'Connor, asking for another interview. It was hard to squeeze him in, but I found a slot early in the evening.

When he duly turned up at the flat, the first thing he did was return my mobile telephone. I thanked him and asked him about the investigation.

He shook his head gloomily. 'Ah, I'd love to tell you, but we're not supposed to talk about it.'

'With a suspect, you mean?'

He looked startled. 'What? Oh, no! You were never a serious suspect, and we ruled you out pretty quick – staff testimony at the Holiday Inn. No, we're just generally not supposed to discuss cases under investigation.' He smiled. 'Lucky for you, we *are* allowed to confirm that we're investigating, and we've been doing a lot of that. You've certainly made trouble for your bosses.'

I shrugged. 'They did it to themselves, really. I mean, I could've told them: if you get caught *in flagrante* doing something unethical, the last thing you want to do is sue the whistleblower. Sack them, maybe, but don't sue. Even if you win you've drawn more attention to the whole business. Threatening to sue a *dying PR officer* – that was just stupid! It got them ten times more bad publicity than if they'd just kept quiet.'

O'Connor grinned. 'So what should they have done?'

'Greenwash themselves. "Mistakes were made in the past, blah blah, *now*, though, we are looking into our timber-buying policy and in future we will be able to provide our customers with *certified* hardwoods from *responsibly farmed* plantations." They don't really even have to change their policy very much: they can get their suppliers to come up with some Mickey Mouse certification and trumpet it loudly as a triumph for environmentalism. The percentage of the public that will take the time to understand what the certification actually involves is so small that they can safely ignore it.'

'Is it doing PR that made you so cynical?'

'I did *their* PR for three years, OK? I used to write that sort of stuff. What was it you wanted to ask me, Inspector?'

He wanted to ask more about the stolen files: like Thomas, the police seemed to have arrived at the suspicion that there was a missing computer disk. I confessed my technophobic reliance on paper.

'Oh,' said O'Connor, clearly disappointed. Then he frowned and asked, 'Did your bosses *know*, though, that you hadn't just copied everything on the computer?'

'Of course not! I didn't intend to *admit* I'd done anything at all; I didn't want the hassle. The first time Ken accused me of taking his files, I pretended I didn't know what he was talking about.'

He nodded as though this made sense to him. 'Don't blame you.'

'I think this might be a bit of a geek test,' I went on. 'A real anorak would just *assume* that I'd copied those files, or emailed them or something. He wouldn't have dreamed of printing them out.'

'And your Mr Norman was a geek?'

I had to think about that a moment. 'Not a real one,' I decided, 'but certainly tending that way. Can you check his computer?'

'No,' said O'Connor quietly. 'It's missing.' He asked a few more questions, confirming details, then thanked me and departed.

On Thursday, when my share of the public's attention was at its height, I received another phone call from Colin Douglas of Griffin Legal. He told me that my accusations were defamatory.

'What accusations are those, Mr Douglas?' I asked sweetly.

'You know perfectly well!'

'Assume I don't.'

A silence. 'In the papers you say—'

'I've told the papers what's happened to me since I blew the whistle on your clients. Are you denying that the events I've described actually occurred?'

'You *implied* . . .'

'I'm not responsible for the *inferences* people draw, Mr Douglas. If you check, you'll see that I haven't "accused" your clients of anything – except of instructing you to sue me if I fail to "cooperate" with them. Are you going to claim *that's* defamatory?'

'The *Daily Mail* says . . .'

'I'm not responsible for the *Daily Mail*, either. Sue *them*, if you like.'

Another silence.

'I'm considering a counter-suit,' I said, on impulse. 'Your clients, or their PR firm, have said that I'm delusional. *That* is certainly false and defamatory. I think I owe it to everyone who's ever suffered from an injury to the brain to make it clear that it does not invalidate everything we say forever after.'

It was an empty threat. Even if I survived long enough to

bring the case to court, I couldn't win: a jury would never feel confident about the distinction between 'suffering from hallucinations' and 'suffering from delusions'. MHD, however, didn't know about the hallucinations, and the threat might worry them enough to make them hesitate about repeating the slur.

Douglas faltered a moment, then exclaimed triumphantly, 'We're not responsible for implications, either!'

'I think it may amount to more than implications, Mr Douglas. I'll get someone to have a look and see, shall I? Was there any point to this call, beyond the attempt to intimidate me?'

'I reject that . . .'

'What would you call it, then?' I snapped, suddenly angry. 'You're calling a woman who's going to fucking *die* in a few months, and threatening to tie up those months with legal action unless she helps your clients suppress some information that makes them look bad. *Real* information, Mr Douglas. You *know* that the documents I leaked are genuine; I'm *sure* you know that. What do you tell yourself about it? That you're just doing your job?'

'Look,' he said, suddenly sounding human and defensive, 'it's not *me*! I'm only a junior partner, and anyway we don't pick and choose cases. I mean, if we did that, there'd be people nobody was willing to defend, and how would you get justice then?'

The lawyers' litany. I supposed, though, that hackneyed as the argument was, it had some truth to it. 'Go away,' I said wearily. 'You want to sue me, go right ahead. It's never going to come to court. If you believe in these things, I'll be answering to a higher authority.'

'I'm sorry,' he said, and ended the call.

As I put the phone down, I wondered why MHD was bothering. They'd already seen that I wasn't going to yield to threats, and they must have realized that I'd be dead before they got a hearing.

I supposed that they kept threatening me for the same reason that they hadn't thought of greenwashing themselves: the concept of remorse was so alien to them that they couldn't even *pretend* to feel it. To them, guilt wasn't a matter of conscience, but of legal assessment; its burden lay in fines, not in feelings. It had to be denied, and anyone who threatened that denial had to be silenced or discredited.

I supposed I should be pleased that they'd decided to say I was delusional: it meant they couldn't turn around and say that I was dishonest, that I was slandering them in revenge because they'd been preparing to sack me for incompetence.

I wasn't pleased, though. I was fed up. I knew perfectly well why they hadn't tried the 'dishonesty' line – because their new PR firm had advised them that punishing a dying woman would make them look heartless. In fact, of course, they *were* heartless, and I was tired of it. I supposed that really I should look into hiring a solicitor to defend myself – but it seemed such a waste of effort! I resented having to think about it at all.

By Thursday afternoon there had been no more attempts to make my life 'hell on earth', and I was beginning to suspect that Ken had been solely responsible for the nastiness. I wondered if he'd *really* been murdered, or if he'd committed suicide. I could imagine that. Just as I could picture him attacking my flat in a red-faced frenzy, I could imagine him hanging himself in a white-faced panic when the police inquired after him. True, criminal damage wasn't that serious an offence – it probably wouldn't even have got him a custodial sentence – but the public shame might have seemed overwhelming to a man like Ken. Summers and O'Connor had been talking about 'homicide', but maybe their investigation was only intended to rule that out.

I started to relax, and even, cautiously, to make plans. I phoned a couple of old college friends, and arranged to spend a weekend in London with them, seeing plays and looking at museums; I suggested to my mother that I'd be home by the end of the month. Then I went through my emails.

The latter was a depressing task: it brought home how many people I'd lost touch with. At school and university I'd been a reasonably social being; during my marriage, many of those contacts had withered. I should have renewed them after the divorce; instead, I'd moved to a new town and a new job and, I now realized, had gone for years without seeing several people I'd once cared about. It was a shock, especially when I tried to work out how many people I *had* been seeing regularly outside work.

Of course, many of my friends had also been Ian's, and Ian had always been the star of every social gathering – lively, extrovert, entertaining. After the split, I hadn't known how to talk to them, so I hadn't wanted to mix in those gatherings any more. Still, I could have made *new* friends. Why on earth had I chosen to live without a social life? As old acquaintances sent notes or emailed to tell me how sorry they were, I wondered how I'd managed to come so far adrift from everything I'd *wanted* from life.

At least I had a social life *now*: I was seeing quite a lot of the Rainforest Trust. Thursday night found us sharing a curry at a local restaurant: Rafi, Nur Rashidah, Thomas, Thomas's girlfriend, and me, laughing together over the popadums as we recounted our publicity triumphs. (Of course Thomas had a girlfriend: such men always do. She was a skinny blonde named Irene who wore an ethnic skirt and a Fairtrade cardigan, and she was in her second year teaching psychology at a large comprehensive. I gathered that Rafi, too, had a girlfriend somewhere, but apparently her position was of a temporary nature, and he had not brought her along.)

As we divvied up the bill, Nur Rashidah shyly suggested that we meet again at her place, so that she could cook us her Malaysian meal. 'I thought, Saturday?'

We all agreed; then, however, I remembered that I had Ian coming.

'Oh!' exclaimed Nur Rashidah, when I explained. 'Oh, of course you must spend time with him.'

The words, and the look – real or imagined – of romantic satisfaction, annoyed me for some reason. 'It's unlikely to be much fun,' I told her bluntly. 'We probably *will* end up quarrelling. I don't want to, but it'll probably happen anyway. I'll probably regret seeing him at all.'

'Oh, no! Of course you must see him. You must make your peace.'

'Must I? And what if I don't?'

She gave me her most earnest look. 'It would hurt you,

when you came to leave this world. I am sure you would regret it.'

'I'd go to hell, would I?'

Nur Rashidah shook her head, shocked. 'No, no! God is great and compassionate: who can make limits to his mercy? I am sure that when we die, he reaches out even to the souls who never knew him. No, Toni. Surely you *want* to make peace with your husband?'

'What I *wanted* never seemed to make much odds when we were married.'

'But now it is different. Before what you wanted belonged to this world; now you say goodbye to it.'

'You don't have to be so blunt about it!' said Thomas uncomfortably.

'She does,' I told him, feeling obscurely relieved. 'She's right.' I grimaced and tried to make a joke of it. 'You know, I always thought that dying would at least mean you didn't have to worry about housework or your relationships any more. I couldn't have been more wrong: it's like moving house and a family crisis rolled into one. I never expected it to be so much *work*.'

Nobody smiled.

On Friday I tidied the flat, set up a folding bed in the study, and ordered the makings of a good meal from the delivery service. It didn't take long, and when I finished it was still only ten in the morning. Ian wouldn't arrive until eight, doing the drive after a full day's work.

I checked my email, wrote responses to a couple of letters, then sat at the computer, staring at the screen. The waterfall came on; above it I could see the ghostly reflection of my face.

Not a bad face, for all the years and the encroaching illness. Wide forehead, long nose, generous mouth – as Ian had termed it, when he loved me. I'd always seen it just as 'big' before that, but after he praised it I took to wearing bright lipstick.

Webster was much possessed by death / And saw the skull beneath the skin.

I looked for the skull, but all I saw was the skin, pale in

this dim reflection, and the direct, challenging eyes. I was flesh and blood for a while longer.

I closed my eyes, imagining Ian's grin and his bright blue eyes. I wondered if we would make love during his visit – and even as I thought of it, I wanted it, wanted that tender delight and oblivious glory one more time. We'd once been lovers, and would soon part forever: why shouldn't we say goodbye with love? Why should we quarrel instead? I didn't want to – but then, I never *had* wanted to. The bitter words had always left raw welts on my heart – the ones I'd spoken no less than the ones I'd heard. I dreaded the evening.

I shut down the computer and got up. There was no point sitting and worrying. I would . . . I would go shopping! After all, it was the middle of November, and I hadn't done a thing about Christmas.

It was Friday morning: Nur Rashidah would be at her lectures. Well, it wouldn't have been fair to drag her around the shops for a kaffir festival, anyway. I would get a taxi.

I shopped extravagantly. I bought an expensive new camera for my brother, an antique herbal for my sister-in-law, a pair of pearl earrings for a friend. I stopped for a cup of coffee, then returned to the fray. I was exhilarated by the sense that the money I spent was Monopoly money, part of a game which soon I would abandon. Late in the afternoon I took another taxi home, and staggered into Canalside festooned with shopping bags, exhausted, struggling with a headache, but happy.

The fire alarm went off while I was in the lift. I sighed, thinking one of the neighbours must have burned a pan again, but when the doors of the lift opened, I found the corridor full of smoke.

I knew at once, but I pretended to myself that I didn't. No one was about – it was still too early for the wage-slaves to be home – and I walked slowly down an empty corridor toward my flat, with the alarm, painfully loud, dinning in my ears. The smoke grew thicker and more acrid. The door I'd had installed only the week before now frowned at me. English oak, still pale and new, locked into place with stainless steel hinges tastefully hidden in the frame and painted white. There was no mark on it, but around it the smoke was thickening visibly, as though condensing from the very air. I touched my fingers to the pale oak, then snatched my hand away again: the wood was scorching hot.

I dared not open the door: I knew the room beyond was full of fire. My books were burning; my CDs melting and blackening, their iridescent plastic yielding bitter tendrils to add to that choking smoke. In the spare room, the bed I'd made up for Ian stood in a fog; my own bed was beginning to char. I stood there in the corridor, with the noise beating against my ears and my eyes stinging with the smoke, and imagined it all.

Something moved at the corner of my eye, and I turned toward it.

It was snowing. The flakes fell in a glittering flurry; the floor of the corridor was already white. I turned back toward the door, and was almost blinded by stinging spindrift. Even as the smoke scored my throat, my eyes reported a blizzard.

I closed my eyes and felt the wetness of tears on my cheeks. I wasn't sure whether I was crying for my flat, for my brain, or simply because of the smoke. I reached out and touched the door again, again snatched my hand back, then fumbled for the wall. I found it and started to stumble back toward the lift. The smoke was growing rapidly worse, and I began to cough, then had to double over as the effort made my head ache. I remembered that you were supposed to stay low when there was a fire, so I dropped to hands and knees, opening my eyes in the hope that the snow would have gone.

It hadn't: the ground was deep-drifted and the air was full of flying spume. I couldn't see the corridor at all. I tried to crawl along it, and banged my head against the wall. I stopped, shaking with horror, then closed my eyes and crawled on, shoulder against the wall. The plaster was smooth against my side, the carpet rough under my hands and knees. The alarm still shrilled, deafening me, sending jagged spikes of pain through my overburdened skull.

If I'd been able to think clearly I would have realized that I was on the wrong side of the corridor for the lift. I wasn't able to, and I crawled past it, past two locked doors, and into the wall at the end of the corridor. I stopped there and huddled against the wall, unable to remember the way back, eyes squeezed shut and hands over my ears. Where were the stairs? Next to the lift, and that was . . . somewhere back there, in the shrieking whiteness. I could no longer tell the difference between the ringing of the alarm and the throbbing of my head. I opened my eyes and stared out into the flying snow. There was a figure there, moving towards me – an indistinct, shrouded figure, shapeless in the blizzard. I was somehow certain that it was Ken, and I screamed.

The next thing I knew my throat and lungs hurt and there was something over my mouth. I fumbled at it, and a man's voice said, 'It's all right,' and gently moved my hand away.

I opened my eyes and blinked muzzily at the face above me. The light was dim, and there was a scent of fire and of damp; the man above me was young, black, helmeted, with some kind of gas mask or breathing apparatus loose around his neck.

'You're all right now,' he told me, patting my hand. 'Just leave the mask on, OK? It's oxygen, 'cause of the smoke inhalation.' He smiled at me reassuringly, a white flash of teeth. 'You're OK now. The fire's out.'

I lay still, breathing painfully, trying to assemble the pieces. Fire, yes: there had been a fire. And I'd tried to run away, but had only got as far as the other end of the corridor. I was still *in* that corridor, lying on the soot-stained carpet, but the fire brigade had arrived and put the fire out. This nice young fireman had *rescued* me. I was desperately, tearfully grateful to him, and I snuffled into the oxygen mask and squeezed his reassuring hand.

After a minute or so another fireman turned up with a stretcher, and he and my first rescuer carried me down to the ground floor – twelve floors, by the stairs, since they were not supposed to use the lift. Outside it was early evening, with the light just beginning to fade. The trees along the canal stood shadowy, half-denuded by the advancing winter, but the water of the canal was a sheet of pink light. The few of my neighbours who'd been home stood in a little knot on the pavement, shivering and looking longingly into the warm, well-lit foyer. There was an ambulance standing by the curb;

my rescuers took me straight out to it. I looked back as they bundled me in, and saw Canalside standing against the darkening sky, the windows of the central stairwell illuminated, the facade pristine. Only my own window, high up on the twelfth floor, looked blackened and gaping.

The ambulance ferried me to the hospital A&E department, where they determined that I was suffering from smoke inhalation – what a surprise! – and debated whether I needed a tube down my throat. They decided I'd be all right with just an oxygen mask, and stuck me in a side room on a trolley while they looked about for a bed.

I lay still for a while, trying not to move my head because that made the ache worse. Perhaps I dozed. Certainly I didn't notice the police arriving: I simply looked up to find them standing there.

It was not fat and friendly O'Connor this time; it was the cold, dark Summers, along with a man in uniform. They both looked at me with misgiving. A hospital nurse, who'd accompanied them, came over to check the oxygen mask, then tested the oxygenation of my blood with a little gadget that clipped on to my fingertip. 'Mrs Lanchester?' she said, with that forced medical cheeriness. 'The police want to ask you a few questions about the fire. Do you feel up to talking to them?'

I pulled off the mask. 'Yes.'

'If you feel short of breath, or you need any help, ring the buzzer,' she instructed me, showing me the little plastic switch. 'Someone will come at once.' She nodded to the policemen and went out.

Summers frowned at me distrustfully. 'We need to know as much as you can tell us about the fire.'

I tried to speak, found my throat full of phlegm, and coughed instead. The uniformed officer glanced round, found a box of tissues, and handed me one.

'Were you in the flat when it caught fire?' Summers asked, when I finally stopped coughing.

'No.' My voice came out hoarse. The coughing had thrust spikes of pain behind my eyes, and I closed them. 'I was out Christmas shopping. I was in the lift, coming home, when the alarm went off. I went up to the door, but it was hot, so I didn't open it. I couldn't . . .' I stopped, remembering the blizzard, and the agonizing pulse of the alarm in my head.

'When would this have been?'

'About four. Maybe a little earlier.' I suddenly remembered all the gifts I'd bought. I couldn't even remember when and where I'd dropped them. 'I had bags full of shopping,' I whispered plaintively. 'Christmas presents. Has anybody found them?'

'We'll ask,' the uniformed policeman offered.

'Thank you.'

'When did you leave the flat?' asked Summers.

I told him; gave him the name of the taxi-firm I'd used; confirmed again that I hadn't entered the flat when I arrived home, and that the door had been closed. Locked? Summers wanted to know. I'd left it that way; I hadn't noticed that anyone had touched it. Damaged? I hadn't noticed; there had been smoke . . . Faced with his distrustful look, I didn't mention the blizzard: I told him that I'd mistaken the way back to the lift because of the smoke and because my head had started to hurt quite badly.

The next question surprised me. 'Did you have fireworks in the flat?'

I stared incredulously, then started coughing again. I shook my head and managed to choke out, 'No!'

'You're sure of that. There weren't any, say, left over from Bonfire Night?'

I mopped my mouth and said hoarsely, 'I haven't been in the mood for *fireworks*, Inspector!' My chest hurt from all that coughing, and my breath was wheezing. I fumbled for the oxygen mask and got it back over my face.

'Did you notice anything odd before you went out? Any strangers, for example, hanging about outside the building?'

I stared again, then pulled the mask down to say I hadn't noticed – but instead started coughing again, badly enough that even Summers looked concerned. I pushed the buzzer to summon the nurse; she did indeed appear at once. Summers, looking uncomfortable, thanked me and left.

The nurse gave me a drink of water and an injection. 'It's just an antihistamine, love. Your throat was irritated by breathing all that smoke, and it's producing all this mucus to protect itself. This will just damp down the reaction. It may make you a bit sleepy.'

It did: I drowsed again, oxygen mask over my face. When I woke once more it was to find Ian standing over me.

He looked the same – perhaps a little bit older, but still the same mop of fair hair, the strong-boned face, the beautiful blue eyes with their perpetual hint of subversive mischief. I gazed at him wordlessly, wondering if he was real, and he came forward and took my hand. 'Toni,' he said softly.

I remembered the first time we'd met, when he'd looked into the audience from the stage of a university theatrical production and invited me out for a drink. I remembered him taking my hand at the registry office where we were married. My anger seemed suddenly unimportant. Yes, he had betrayed my hopes, exploited me, but there had been love. It had been flawed and imperfect, but it had been real: I would not die without having known what love was like. I squeezed his hand, and he leaned down and kissed me on the forehead.

'My poor Toni!' he murmured, stroking my hair. 'Couldn't they even find you a hospital bed?'

I pulled down the oxygen mask. 'What time is it?'

'Half past nine. How long have you been here?'

'Dunno. Since five?' My throat felt much easier. 'When did you get here?'

'Here at the hospital, about ten minutes ago. I went to your flat around eight, like we agreed, and it was burned out and full of policemen. God, Toni, you scared me! What have you got yourself into?'

'I bought stuff for us to have for dinner,' I told him miserably. 'I had everything all set up.'

'Look, look, don't worry! What hotels are for, yah?'

'I'm sorry.'

'Oh, darling heart, don't worry! I can get a hotel. Have you really been sitting here since *five*? They should've got you a bed!'

'Get a hotel for both of us,' I told him. 'I don't want to stay here. I want to go home.'

'Home's burned out,' he said. 'I can get a hotel, though. You sure you don't need to stay here?'

'I want to get away from here,' I told him honestly. 'I'm not ready to die quite yet.'

Ebony
Diospyros ebenum
West Africa

Conservation status unclear – 'data deficient'

Nine

Ian and I ended up back at the Holiday Inn. It was late when we arrived, and we were frazzled from coping with medical bureaucracy, so we didn't do anything except collapse into the king-sized bed. In the morning, though, in the pre-dawn grey, he reached across the bed, and I turned on to my side and put my arms around him, and he sighed.

We made love, slowly and with immense tenderness. I almost started coughing a couple of times, but managed not to. I didn't want to do anything to disturb the sweet pleasure, the release of all my anger and bitterness. I knew – I think we both knew – that it would be the last time. I had taken care not to ask him if there was some other woman now: I was quite certain that the answer was yes.

We went back to sleep afterwards, waking again when it was light. Ian ordered breakfast from room service – I could not go down to the hotel restaurant, since I had nothing to wear except the clothes I'd worn the day before, and they were filthy and reeked of smoke. We ate croissants and jam from a tray on the bedside table, Ian in pajamas and me in his dressing gown – he, of course, had an overnight bag. Ian promised to do some shopping for me as soon as we'd eaten.

My mobile rang while I was finishing my coffee.

It was Thomas. He had heard a report about the fire on the local radio, and he wanted to check that I was OK. I told him I'd been treated for smoke inhalation and was in a hotel, and he said 'Wow!'

'What about your flat?' he then asked anxiously. 'How badly was it damaged? Will you be able to go back there?'

'I don't know.' I thought of that scorching-hot door and blackened window, and added, 'I doubt it.'

There was a silence. I wondered why I wasn't more upset.

The break-in had reduced me to tears; the destruction of all my earthly goods just left me feeling tired. Was it just that I was still numb, or was it because I'd started to resign myself to the loss of all things earthly?

'Who is it?' asked Ian, frowning at me over his own coffee cup. At the same time, Thomas said hesitantly, 'Is this . . . is it still because of what you gave us?'

'A friend,' I told Ian, and incautiously told Thomas, 'Yes. That is . . . I don't know. The police have . . .'

'Can I help? If you need a room you could stay at my place.'

'I'm sure that's not necessary. I was intending to go stay with my mother soon anyway.'

Even as I said it, I wondered. Would it be *safe* to stay with her? If the make-your-life-hell campaign followed me to her door, what would be the result? She was seventy, and very much attached to her house and her possessions. The burglary and the arson attack had been devastating to me: for her they would be . . .

Not fatal; her heart was still strong. Worse than fatal, in a way. An invasion of her home would strike against her confidence, her belief that she could still deal with the world; it would make her neurotic, vulnerable, home-bound.

'What's going on?' asked Ian.

'Ssh! Not you, Thomas. Look, I need to talk to the police. I need to discuss the situation with them and get advice. I'll get back to you afterwards.'

'OK. Just . . . just let me know if there's anything I can do to help, OK?'

I ended the call, then looked up at Ian, who was watching me with an arch look. 'Thomas?'

'Oh, for heaven's sake! Thomas is the environmental activist who runs the website for the organization I gave those letters to. He feels guilty about all the trouble I've had, and he's offering to help.'

'He damn well *should* feel guilty! Toni, was that fire arson?'

'I don't know.'

'That means "yes", doesn't it? Shit. What have you got yourself into?'

'I don't *know*!'

He looked at me resentfully, as though I'd embarked on another rant about his laziness.

'I thought I knew,' I told him slowly. 'I thought the company was angry and my boss was trying to get revenge on me for wrecking his career. That made sense. I didn't like it, but it made sense. Now, though, it's got weird. That fire – that's over the top. I can't imagine the company wanting anything to do with it. And Ken's dead.'

'Ken?'

'My boss.'

'The one whose career you wrecked?'

'Yeah, him. I took the stuff off his computer. I think he's the one who wrecked my flat and posted my picture on the porn site. I don't *know* that – the police haven't told me anything – but it just *feels* right.'

Ian shook his head unhappily. 'Why'd you go work for people like that?'

'What was I supposed to object to at the interview? They're a *furniture* company, not arms dealers! The management culture isn't something you pick up on right away. And I wanted to get away. You know why that was.'

'It wasn't *my* fault!'

I nearly answered 'Yes it *was*!' but I managed to restrain myself. 'It's done now,' I said instead.

'And this boss is *dead*?' Ian asked, after a moment.

I nodded. 'The police came round asking about it, because he'd told people he wanted to speak to me. He was found dead in his house – that was in the paper – but I don't know how he died. I've been trying to tell myself he committed suicide because he was about to get caught over the break-in and he was ashamed, but the police were calling it a *homicide* investigation. And . . .'

'What?' Ian prompted when I trailed off.

'Ken was almost hysterical about what I'd done. He screamed about how I'd destroyed him, and he kept trying to ask me something – but I don't know *what*, because I wouldn't listen. Thomas thinks he must've believed I copied his whole documents folder, that he wanted to know how much I'd passed on. The police seem to think that was possible. In which case, the whole thing is stupid, because I didn't copy his documents on to disk; I just printed out what I found on a quick raid.'

'The written word!' observed Ian sympathetically.

'Yah. It never even occurred to me to copy the disk.' I was silent a moment, then moved on to the detail that had been rubbing a sore place in my thoughts. 'Ken had a daughter. She and her mother found the body when they were dropping her off at the house for the weekend; it was in the paper. I feel dreadful about it.'

'*You're* not the one who killed him,' Ian pointed out. 'Maybe he was blackmailing somebody.'

I stared at him, and everything fell into place.

I telephoned Detective O'Connor. I tried to persuade Ian to go out and buy me some clothes first, but he was reluctant to go.

'Just talk to the police first. I don't want to leave you on your own without knowing you'll be safe.'

I could have pointed out the absurdity of this when he'd left me on my own for the previous three years and was planning to go back to London the next day, but I didn't; I phoned, and let him listen to the conversation.

O'Connor seemed genuinely pleased to hear from me. 'We were just about to go round the hospital again. John told me he saw you last night, and you looked pretty rough.'

'I was feeling pretty rough at the time. But I'm out of hospital now. Inspector, I . . .'

'Ah, that's great to hear! Where are you?'

'Back at the Holiday Inn.'

'We'll come see you there, then.'

'Good. Look, I've been thinking. One of the things I took out of Ken's computer was a financial spreadsheet – I told you that, didn't I?'

'Ah . . . no. I don't think you did. *Letters*, you said.'

'There was a spreadsheet, too. I'm *sure* I told you they'd contributed money.'

'You did, but . . . a spreadsheet?'

'With payments and account numbers. The Rainforest Trust sent it to Malaysia. The thing is, Ken wasn't *in* finance. It wasn't something he should have had. At the time I thought maybe he'd done some digging to confirm suspicions of his own, but now I wonder – that is, my ex, who's visiting, wondered – if he could've been blackmailing somebody.'

There was a silence. 'Right,' O'Connor said at last. 'Right, uh, that's possible.' I understood instantly that he and his colleague had suspected blackmail for days.

'I'm sorry!' I said, chagrined. 'I should have told you about this before.'

'No, no! You did mention it: *we* should've followed up.' He sighed. 'We were assigned to investigate the homicide, though, not your business with the furniture company. Takes a while to know what's relevant. Do you still have this spreadsheet?'

'I gave my print-out to the Rainforest Trust, and they passed it on to their associates in Malaysia. I have a copy, though, on my computer.'

Another pause. 'The computer in your flat? It survived?'

'Oh.' The destruction suddenly hit me, and I clutched my mobile helplessly. 'Oh, I . . . I don't know.'

'We'll check, OK?' O'Connor said gently. 'You know, it may have come out of the fire intact. It was in that study at the end of your hall, wasn't it? The worst of the damage was in the main room.'

'You've looked?'

'Yeah. The, uh, preliminary report indicated arson, so I went and had a look. It's pretty bad. I'm sorry.'

'Your colleague was talking about *fireworks*.' That now seemed so outlandish I wondered if I'd imagined it.

O'Connor sighed. 'Yeah. It looks like somebody shot out your window with an air rifle, then lobbed some fireworks through it.'

I tried to envisage it, but couldn't. 'I'm on the twelfth floor!'

'Yeah. Probably they doctored one of the firework mortars a bit, fired a couple of shots with a water balloon or something first, to get the range. A lady on the seventh floor remembers the thumps of something hitting the building; she says she went and looked out the window, but didn't see anything. She decided it must've been a bird. She heard the

fireworks going off a bit later – several people heard those –
but nobody thought anything about it at the time. People are
always letting off fireworks at this time of year.'

'A *mortar*?'

'Just a firework one. You know some fireworks are mortar
shells, don't you?'

'No,' I admitted. 'I just go "Ooo, aah".'

'Oh. Well, normally the mortar's just a cardboard tube. We
think whoever did this used something a bit fancier, but maybe
it was only some kind of pipe. Could be they were familiar
with military mortars; could be they've just played around with
fireworks before.' O'Connor sighed. 'It's not going to be easy
to trace. This time of year there are fireworks everywhere. And
nobody seems to have seen the guys letting them off.'

'That's weird.'

'No, not really. We think they were probably on the other
side of the canal from you. There's an office car park which
is hidden from the street by the office, and hidden from your
place by all those trees and bushes along the canal. We're
still asking in the office, but the place is soundproofed and
double-glazed, and the people there all say they were very
busy . . . If your computer *is* out of order, is there any other
way we can get a copy of this spreadsheet?'

'There should be.' It was a relief to move away from the
topic of the fire. 'Like I said, Thomas Holden at the Rainforest
Trust sent copies to their partner organizations all over southeast Asia. He must be able to get a copy for you.'

'Thanks. We'll ask him. OK, we'll sort that out, then come
and get your statement about the fire, if you're up to it. Could
you see us at about eleven?'

With the promise that the police would be arriving soon, Ian
was willing to go and buy some clothes for me. Alone in
the hotel room, I showered, then sat down on the bed in Ian's
dressing gown. My reflection watched me from the mirror,
wet hair dark, face pale and haggard. What now?

Inspector O'Connor had said my flat was 'pretty bad'. I
wondered what he considered bad. I remembered my last
glance of Canalside: the blackened window gaping from the
pristine front.

For the first time, I thought to wonder if anyone *else* had been hurt by the fire. There had been that knot of people on the pavement, waiting to go back in. Canalside catered mainly to other professional people, who would have been at work, but there were one or two families, and there would probably have been a couple of residents off sick or working from home. Had anyone else been injured or lost property because some unknown person wanted to punish me?

I would have to ask the police. I would have to go over to the flat myself, to see if anything could be salvaged. I would have to find somewhere else to stay. I would have to contact the insurance company.

I was so *tired*, though. Maybe I should ask Ian to drive me home, to my mother's. I could give up, let others take care of me, slip back into the role of child . . .

. . . Until it was time to go to the hospital and die?

No. I'd begun a fight casually and in ignorance, but the cause had turned out to be good, and the enemies powerful and malign. It was a thing worth doing. I would not give up and die, not yet. I sat up to begin the struggle with the insurance company.

The battery on my mobile was low. I switched to the hotel phone. The recharger for my phone had been in the lounge, and I didn't know when I'd be able to replace it.

The insurance news was depressing. I had yet to get the pay-out for the break-in, and the insurers weren't at all happy to hear from me again so soon. They wouldn't even accept my word that there *had* been a fire: they wanted policy numbers and an incident number, which, of course, I didn't have. They did, however, agree to pick up the bill for a hotel 'for an evaluation period of a week' once I'd provided them with evidence that I was indeed insured with them and was now homeless.

I was relieved to hear it. My bank balance had been sinking alarmingly, and there would be no more salary cheques. I still had the credit card, of course, and the money from cashing in my pension should arrive before too long – but still, I did not want to have worry about overdrafts, on top of everything else.

*   *   *

Ian turned up with clothes for me only two minutes before the police arrived at the hotel. I was still investigating his purchases when Summers phoned up from reception. I told them I would meet them in the lobby in ten minutes and dressed hurriedly. Ian had bought some impractical sexy underclothes, but the dress he'd found was nice, a simple sheath in dusky rose, with a little jacket. He'd always had a good sense of my style. Looking at my reflection in the mirror I decided it would pass – if I had some make-up, which of course I did not.

To hell with it. I was a dying woman, and homeless to boot: I was entitled to look haggard.

Ian escorted me down to the lobby, very gentlemanly and solicitous. Summers and O'Connor were sitting at one of the glass coffee tables; they stood up to greet me, and gave Ian wary looks. He smiled and held out his hand. 'Ian Wilson. Toni and I used to be married, and I've come up this weekend to help her out.'

The men shook hands; Summers was now frowning. 'Have we met?' he asked Ian.

Ian smiled complacently. 'You see much theatre?'

Summers stared at him a moment longer, then nodded sharply. 'You played the journalist in *Brandenburg Gate.*'

'Oh, yeah, you did!' exclaimed O'Connor, impressed. 'That was really good!'

Ian was put out: that had been a television role, and he far preferred to be recognized from his theatrical perform-ances. He accepted the accolade, however, with a gracious smile.

The detectives were evidently unsure of how to treat Ian. Was he my next of kin, and entitled to sit in – or was he an extraneous person, to be excluded? Ian insinuated himself by offering to fetch coffee – coffee-providers are rarely dismissed. He went off to the bar.

O'Connor sat down, then collected up an assortment of shopping bags which had been tucked out of sight next to the hotel's large leather-upholstered sofa. 'They found these outside your flat,' he informed me. 'I think they're yours?'

It was my abandoned Christmas shopping. I'd never expected to see it again, and I took the bags incredulously,

looked through them, found everything intact, and tried –
unsuccessfully – not to cry. O'Connor patted his pockets for
a hankie, but couldn't find one. Ian, returning, gave me one
of the flimsy paper napkins which came with the coffee. I
wiped my eyes, blew my nose, and thanked O'Connor. Then
I had to cough.

Summers was impatient with the delay. He had a statement from me already half-prepared, and he began the interrogation while I was still mopping myself with a second
napkin. Had I noticed anyone hanging about the building on
Friday? Had I noticed any odd noises or events that day or
the day before? Could I confirm when I'd left the flat and
when I'd returned?

At last satisfied, he read out the statement and I agreed
with it and signed it. He handed it to O'Connor, who tucked
it in the ubiquitous briefcase.

'Just a moment,' I said as they prepared to leave. 'I need
some advice, please.'

'What she *needs* is some protection,' said Ian forcefully.

I hadn't objected to him sitting in on the interview, but at
this I gave him a quelling look. What I needed was no longer
his business.

'All I'm doing is stating the obvious!' protested Ian. 'I
mean, Christ, first it's a break-in, then threats, and now an
arson attack! Do you have to get *shot* before you're entitled
to some help?'

Summers gave me a distrustful look, but sat down again.
O'Connor smiled. 'Aren't you planning to protect the lady
yourself, Mr Wilson?'

'I have to be back in London on Monday,' Ian replied,
without the least embarrassment. 'Got rehearsals at the
National Theatre.'

'It's not his job any more,' I told the police drily. 'This
was just a goodbye visit. Look, I don't know if I need
protection or not, but I *do* know that I need advice. You
haven't told me anything about Ken's death or what you
think has been going on, and I haven't asked: that's your
business, and I've been happy to let you get on with it.
Now, though, I'm homeless, I'm going to have to rely on
other people – and I don't want to land on them if I'm

likely to bring disaster down after me. Was anybody else hurt in the fire yesterday?'

O'Connor shook his head. 'Don't you worry about that. There's smoke damage to some of the other flats and the corridors, but you were the only one sent to hospital. That building has a good fire safety set-up, and the fire brigade came running as soon as the alarms went off. They're wired straight to the local fire station.'

I let out an unsteady breath, deeply relieved. 'Am I likely to be attacked again?'

There was a moment of silence, and then Summers said slowly, 'In my view, no. I don't think it was an accident that the arson attack occurred while you were out: I believe it was intended to destroy evidence, not cause injury.'

I stared at him a moment, thinking this through.

'She'd been out for hours when the fire started,' Ian objected. 'They couldn't have known she'd be gone that long.'

I held up a hand to shush him. 'You think someone was watching the flat, and noticed when I left?' That was a creepy thought.

Summers nodded. 'It's true you were out a long time,' he admitted, 'longer than they had any right to expect – but maybe their attack took longer than they expected, too. They may have had trouble breaking the window, or getting their mortar to work.'

'You think they set fire to my flat to destroy a *mythical* computer disk? They could've burned the whole place down!'

'They probably knew the fire could be contained. They knew which window was yours, after all. They knew, too, that they couldn't just shove a burning rag through your door – that's the preferred method. I think probably they were familiar with the building.'

It made my skin crawl. I should have seen the watchers, hanging about the entrance to Canalside or coming in to inspect my new door. They peopled my imagination now: black-clad men in parked cars, sinister Malaysian strangers in dark glasses. The plain truth, though, was that I hadn't noticed anyone.

'Your break-in wasn't the same guys,' O'Connor told me.

'Ken Norman was responsible for that, just like you thought. His fingerprints are on one of the CD cases, and we found your computer at his house.'

'Oh!' It was what I'd suspected, but to have it confirmed was unexpectedly shocking. I *knew* Ken – and now I knew I must have figured in his sexual fantasies. Strange assumption – that criminals are dangerous aliens, and not people we know and work with every day. 'Was it Ken who sent me that note, too?'

'I suppose you're entitled to know how things stand, for your own protection,' Summers said reluctantly. 'Our current theory, then, is this: we suspect that Mr Norman was engaged in blackmail. We believe he had information which was highly embarrassing to his employers, and perhaps to others associated with them. When you leaked some of that information, his victims became extremely angry and alarmed. He was frightened, and he may also have been anxious to know how much information you'd actually found: that, we think, is the reason he broke into your flat. Posting your details on that porn site – that was an act of revenge, pure and simple. The threatening note you received, though, that *doesn't* seem to have been from Mr Norman – at least our experts say it isn't in his handwriting and doesn't match any notebook, pen or envelope he's known to have possessed. It may well have been from a victim, trying to intimidate you into handing over information he believed you had in your possession.

'What information Mr Norman had, we don't know. We found *your* computer at his house, but his own is missing, and the night he died someone broke into his office and removed his work computer as well. The letters you showed us aren't enough to account for what's happened. Whether this spreadsheet might be, I can't say. My guess, though, is that Mr Norman had something which amounted to a smoking gun, that it hasn't been released, and that somebody fears it might be. What I'd recommend, Ms Lanchester, is that you make it clear to your media contacts that you never had anything except three documents, all of which are already in the public domain. If you do that, I'd say you're unlikely to need any protection.'

I nodded, relieved. It sounded as though a confession of my reliance on paper would be enough to let me go home safely. 'The financial spreadsheet – have you got a copy of it?'

O'Connor sighed. 'Not yet. We couldn't get your computer to work. We took it in to the station, to see if anybody there can fix it, but they're not optimistic – they think there must have been an electrical short or surge or something which fried the hard drive. We've got in touch with your friend Mr Holden, though. He's going to try to get a copy from his friends in Malaysia – once he gets his own computers back from the anti-terrorist squad.'

'They still have them?' I asked in surprise. 'They told me the inquiry was closed last Monday!'

O'Connor grinned. 'Ah, but Mr Holden has to arrange to come and *fetch* the computers; the anti-terrorist lads are far too grand to deliver them! And it seems that Mr Holden is so deeply green he won't own a car, because he can't stand the thought of adding his own little bit to global warming. He told us he's been meaning to borrow a car to fetch his computers home, but he's been busy and he hasn't managed it. Of course, it hasn't been urgent to him, what with you letting him use your computer whenever he wants to. John and I are going to have a word with the anti-terrorists lads, see if we can't get them to give the poor man his computers back.'

'He could've borrowed *my* car.'

'Oh, he wouldn't trouble you,' said O'Connor. 'He thinks you're a saint, and he's all on fire to defend you.'

'Is this the Thomas who phoned this morning?' Ian asked suspiciously.

'Yes,' I said in disgust. 'Ian, we're *divorced* – though for that matter, I'm almost old enough to be Thomas Holden's mother!'

'You never look it,' O'Connor told me gallantly.

When the police had gone, I asked Ian to take me over to Canalside to see what could be salvaged; I hoped that I might at least find my insurance policy.

It was a grey day, with heavy clouds that threatened rain.

We parked on the street outside the building, under the denuded trees. I looked up at Canalside: it seemed to be back to normal, apart from my own blackened window.

'You sure you're up to this?' asked Ian.

I nodded and got out of the car.

We rode up in the lift in silence. My oak door still seemed disconcertingly undamaged, but there were noises from behind it.

If Ian hadn't been there I would have slunk off; as it was, I reminded myself that the police must have been in and out of the apartment ever since the fire was put out, and unlocked the door. It opened to a reek of fire and startled stares from the forensics team busy in the blackened ruin of the lounge. A stout man in dungarees and a face mask hurried over to us. 'You can't come in!' he declared angrily. 'Scene of a crime!'

'It's *my* flat!' I protested, staring past him. The furniture hadn't been completely consumed: it slumped in its accustomed arrangement, charred frames supporting trailing brown lumps of scorched kapok where the upholstery had been burned away. The books were still in the bookcases, but their spines were black; the CDs were a twisted block inside a charred case. The Renoir print on the wall must have stayed up through the worst of the fire, because there was a neat rectangle of lighter-coloured paint where it had been; the print itself was a heap on the floor below. Everything was soaked, presumably by the water used to extinguish the fire, and it stank of ash and burned plastic. The broken window gaped open to the cloudy day, and the room was so cold that the three people in it wore coats.

'*Your* flat?' asked the investigator, taken aback. After a moment he added, in a more polite tone, 'Can you show me some ID?'

I produced my driving licence from my handbag, and he dithered between officiousness and pity. 'I'm not supposed to let you in till we've finished, but . . .'

'I need to get my insurance details – and some clothes, if anything's survived.'

Officialdom yielded: we were allowed in, but told to stay out of the lounge. I walked slowly down the corridor to my study. The damage there was much less severe: everything was covered with a thick grime from the smoke, but the desk and filing cabinet seemed intact, and when I opened the cabinet drawers, the papers seemed to be unharmed. I found the insurance policy, then stood a moment trying to think if there was anything else I should fetch.

'Deeds to the flat?' suggested Ian. 'I mean, maybe you could sell it back to whoever it is that owns this place. Let *them* worry about cleaning it.'

'Good thought!' I rummaged in the files.

We emerged from the study with a thick pile of documents and went on to my bedroom. This had suffered much more than the study – it was immediately adjacent to the lounge, and the heat had been enough to warp the lampshades – but I found a suitcase more or less intact in the top of my wardrobe. I dumped the papers in it, and looked at my clothes. The things in the top layers of the chest of drawers were singed-looking and spotted, but the lower layers looked as though they might be all right after a wash; similarly, in the wardrobe, the items furthest from the lounge wall seemed usable. I packed them in the case and went into the bathroom.

Everything there was grimed with smoke; the tiles had cracked and the polycarbonate shower screen had turned white and curled like the petal of a flower. The ebony box beside the sink where I stored my cosmetics had become a ruin of plastic containers and coloured grease – though, oddly, the box itself was undamaged. It was a pretty thing, a gift from a friend who'd been to visit Kenya, so I tipped the wreckage into the bin and kept the box. I considered putting my toothbrush in it, then looked at the stained brush and decided that it would be better simply to buy a new one. I collected my jewellery box from its place in the second drawer down, though, and was relieved to find it not much damaged. I glanced round the ruin, trying to think, then went to the bathroom cabinet and took out the co-codamol and the dexamethasone.

The label on the latter told me it needed to be stored at less than 25 degrees. I would have to telephone the hospital for a fresh prescription. For a moment that little chore – one more damned thing to do – seemed almost overwhelming, and I had to stop and stand still a moment, staring into the cracked and smoke-fogged mirror.

'You can come stay with me, if you like,' Ian volunteered hesitantly.

I looked round at him, startled, and saw that he meant it. 'What would your girlfriend think of that?'

He winced. 'We were *married*. You're in trouble, and you've got a terminal illness. If she can't put up with it, to hell with her!'

Through the doorway behind him I saw the forest: the tree roots curling across the floor, the deep carpet of decaying leaves. Sunlight filtered down through green, and made patches of brightness in the heavy air, where the wings of butterflies flashed.

I shook my head, trying not to look at it. 'Ian, it's very sweet of you, and I'm touched – but no. I don't want to have to deal with that. I'll stay here for another week or so, in the hotel, and then go home to my mum. She's been after me to come home for a couple of weeks already.'

He nodded resignedly, then reached over, pulled me close, and kissed me, and at once the trees were all about us. 'You were the sun and the moon to me,' he said, his voice thick with tears. 'I only wish we'd been wise.'

Camphor Laurel
Cinnamonum camphora
Southeast Asia

Invasive in Australia

Ten

On the way back to the hotel, my phone rang. It was the local paper: somebody had just realized that the minor fire at Canalside might be part of a bigger story, and the *Evening Telegraph* scented a scoop. I agreed to do an interview, and a gauche young reporter duly showed up at the hotel half an hour later.

I wasn't at my best: I was feeling very tired by the time she arrived, and my head was pounding. I hadn't forgotten Inspector Summers' injunction to make it plain to the world that I had no incriminating documents in reserve, but I didn't know how to do so coherently. In the end I didn't say much beyond yes, I'd been made homeless by an arson attack, and yes the police were investigating: could I go and lie down now?

Ian, however, charmed the young woman. When the story eventually came out (Monday evening – the *Evening Telegraph* didn't rise to a Sunday edition) he emerged heroic, rushing from rehearsals at the National Theatre to the aid of his stricken ex-wife, fearlessly denouncing those who had attacked me. He got himself into the photo, too, looking noble with a protective hand on my shoulder. It irritated me, even at the time, but I let it pass. That's what Ian was like. I'd divorced him now, and there was no point in getting upset about it.

I knew that one interview would provoke more, but I was too tired to think about it. I took some of the doubtful dexamethasone and a couple of co-codamol and lay down.

Nur Rashidah phoned while I was just dozing off. She'd just heard about the fire, from Thomas, and she was horrified and very worried. I snarled at her that I was all right, and told her I was trying to rest.

I managed to rouse myself enough to have dinner with Ian, though only in the hotel restaurant. He told me all about the play at the National Theatre, and about several other plays as well. His career seemed to be going much better, now that financial necessity compelled him to join the scrum for the less appetising roles – though he didn't admit that, of course. I enjoyed the evening. He was full of the usual exaggerated theatrical anecdotes, and made me laugh. I could remember why I'd married him.

He wanted to make love again afterwards, but I declined. Now that her existence had been acknowledged, the other woman came between us. Besides, my head had started to hurt quite badly.

It hurt even more next morning. I didn't want to get out of bed, but at six a.m. I had to, in order to be sick. I staggered into the bathroom door, bruising my shoulder, and barely found the toilet in time. Vomiting sent hammer-blows through my skull with each heave. I couldn't even see straight: the whole world was blurred and doubled. I very much regretted not making time to get that fresh prescription the day before.

Ian was kinder and more helpful than I'd believed he ever could be. During our marriage he'd recoiled from sickness and filth, and he'd regarded other people's illnesses with impatience. (He'd expected infinite indulgence when he was unwell himself, of course.) Now he was all gentleness. He washed my face and put me back to bed with a damp cloth over my eyes; he telephoned NHS Direct, and then the hospital; he ferried me to Accident & Emergency, sat with me during the inevitable wait for treatment, and held my hand while I was injected with anti-nausea stuff and some intravenous dexamethasone-analogue. Then he ferried me back to the hotel and went to collect the fresh prescriptions for me – there were two of the things now, dexamethasone and a morphine-based painkiller.

The drugs helped. I'd been taking the dexamethasone religiously since Dr Hillman first prescribed it, but I'd privately doubted whether it was actually doing anything. Clearly, it had, and my condition must have deteriorated since the diagnosis. That smoke-shrimp behind my ear had grown fat, gorging on the blood-rich substance of my brain.

Ian continued to be extraordinarily helpful throughout that Sunday. He took some of my smoke-scented clothes to a laundrette and dropped others off at a dry cleaners in a supermarket; he got a new recharger for my phone; he fetched me soup, made tea, and generally looked after me as tenderly as a mother. In the evening, though, he went back to London.

'I hate to leave you,' he said, but he did. I had known he would, and made no protests: what he had done was more than I'd ever expected. I promised to keep him posted, and he promised to come and visit again – 'at your mother's, if you do go there. If she can still stand me, that is.' My mother adored him, and he knew it.

I was feeling well enough to go down to the hotel lobby to say goodbye, and when he had gone I stood there looking out the window for a little while, wondering if I would ever see him again.

The national press didn't bother me that Sunday: presumably no one else had picked up on my connection to the fire. I hadn't contacted any of the people I knew in the national media, either – I'd been too ill, and too preoccupied with Ian. Monday morning, though, seemed a good time to get back to work. I needed to do what Summers had advised.

I set out to draft a statement, only to realize that I had nothing to draft it on except the hotel's complimentary stationery. Technophobe though I was, it had been years since I prepared anything on paper, and I found it difficult. (My vision kept doubling, too, which scared me.) I wrote out a bald account of the situation as Summers and O'Connor had reported it – then scratched it out. I could not say that Ken was suspected of blackmail, not while the matter was still under investigation: it would be libellous, or prejudicial or something, and it would probably be very distressing to his daughter and his ex-wife.

I tried again, and managed to produce something that made it sound as though Masterpiece Home Design was directly responsible for the fire. That would certainly add fuel to their law suit, and I didn't even believe it! I tried a third time, and ran out of paper halfway through. I telephoned Nur Rashidah.

She exclaimed with relief when she recognized my voice, and asked, with deep concern, how I was. My conscience reproached me, and I apologized for my brusqueness on the Saturday.

'Oh, do not think of it!' she cried. 'You have suffered so much!'

'Suffer' wasn't the verb I would have used; it was a surprise to realize that I might actually be entitled to it.

I told Nur Rashidah what Summers had said about the fire and his advice about making it clear that I did not have any revelations in reserve, then explained my difficulties in drafting the statement. She suggested that she take me over to the Rainforest Trust.

'I think this would be easier for you to do on a computer, yes? And we have the computers again! The police brought them back on Saturday. Thomas says that the Detective Inspector who is in charge of the investigation brought them himself!'

'O'Connor?' I asked curiously. 'Or Summers?'

Nur Rashidah hesitated, and I remembered that she'd scarcely met either man. 'Never mind!' I told her. I was sure it had been O'Connor, anyway. Summers, like 'the anti-terrorist lads', was too grand to play delivery man. I wished I could escape the conviction that the less sympathetic of the pair was also much the cleverer.

Nur Rashidah went to fetch the car and I lay down to rest while I waited for her to collect me.

I thought about her *fetching* the car. Anyone else would have simply taken charge of the machine and parked it at their own residence, but to Nur Rashidah it was *my* car, and so it sat at Canalside, waiting for me and my heirs and assigns to climb into it, while Nur Rashidah went to fetch it on her bicycle, then came to collect me. I would have to give her the Porsche; she had more than earned it. I wondered if I could do that just by filling out the relevant section of the car registration document, or if I needed to consult a lawyer.

She was a sweet girl. I wondered what she'd do with her microbiology degree. Go home to work in a medical laboratory? Did Malaysia provide opportunities to female microbiologists? Probably it did; it always seemed much more enlightened and tolerant than most developing countries.

I wondered if she had a boyfriend back home, or if she would have a marriage arranged for her on her return. I tried to imagine her as a blushing bride. I couldn't make the leap – though I could easily see her as a devoted wife, making excuses for some conceited fool of a husband, who condescended to her and neglected her.

Maybe she'd do better than that. Maybe she'd marry some earnest young doctor, and they'd live happily ever after, working nobly together to heal the world's ills. I hoped so. Lying there, waiting for her to collect me, I wished for the happiness of *everyone* whose life touched mine – and I knew that the world would frustrate my wishes, for some or for all of them. Happiness is rare.

Nur Rashidah arrived at the hotel in the Porsche, and we drove over to the Rainforest Trust's shabby little office. Seeing it a second time brought home to me what a shoestring operation I'd managed to get myself involved with. I asked about the charity shop. Surely the organization had better sources of income than second-hand books and bric-a-brac?

'Oh, yes, we are a registered charity!' she told me proudly. 'We have *many* donors, in Malaysia and Indonesia and here in Britain. They pay for our work there, and they pay Thomas's salary. But there is not much money for running the office. Selling things helps very much with that.'

Shoestring, I thought resignedly – but effective, it seemed, at least in its Asian homelands. I went in, clutching my scribbled sheet of hotel stationery.

Nur Rashidah had evidently warned Thomas that I was coming, because he was expecting me. He had found an extra chair somewhere and had even made some attempt to clear up his desk. His computer sat proudly on the pine surface, still trailing a police *Evidence* sticker. I asked if he'd managed to get a copy of the financial spreadsheet for Summers and O'Connor.

'I printed it out as soon as I had the machine set up again,' he assured me. 'And I told our partners that they were interested, and got contact numbers for the Malaysian police.'

'The Malaysian police have a copy of the spreadsheet?'

'Oh, yeah! See, they set up an investigation right after the killings, but they couldn't find enough evidence to prosecute anybody – at least, they *said* they couldn't. You never know, in cases like that, if it's just that the witnesses have been got at, or whether the problem's with the police or the prosecutors. Anyway, they hadn't officially closed the investigation, even though it had gone cold. Our guys just handed your documents to the relevant official and asked him to check them out.'

'And will he?'

'Absolutely! Our guys say that particular official has a really good reputation, but he'd have to do something even if he was crooked, or people would want to know why. The massacre was a *big thing* in Sarawak; politicians were falling over themselves to denounce the killers and promise speedy justice. To tell the truth, I think probably the problem *was* with the witnesses. I mean, you can see it. Would you testify against murderers when they're walking around loose in your own village?'

I thought about that. 'I don't see how anything I gave you would help with that!'

'Oh, no!' Nur Rashidah interjected. 'It changes everything.'

'The guys who did the actual killing, and the guys who organized them, are relying on somebody for protection,' Thomas elaborated. 'Maybe it's just the logging company, or maybe there's somebody in the state government as well. If their protector is strong, they'll keep their mouths shut – but if they see that he's in trouble, they'll be tempted to inform on him, to save their own skins.'

'I *see*.' I hadn't thought about any of this before; I'd been too wrapped up in my own affairs. I wondered now about the accounts on that spreadsheet. What were they? A logging company's slush fund? A politician's secret bribe stash? A multinational's payment of blood money? Was it the owner of one of those accounts who'd arranged for my flat to burn?

I'd have to leave that to the police, both British and Malaysian. What I needed to do was make it clear that the spreadsheet was my best shot, and I'd fired it.

Thomas let me take over his computer, and I typed in my half-drafted statement, completed it, and went over it. I would have liked to consult Rafi about libel again, but he was at work, so I contented myself with being cautious.

I'd lost my email address book – again – and I had to look up my contacts by the titles of the papers they worked for, and despatch copies of my statement 'for the attention of . . .' It took some time, but Thomas sat quietly reading papers while I worked, and did not press me to hurry. Nur Rashidah went off to a lecture. The shop had one customer, who bought a second-hand paperback for fifty pence – a great help with office expenses, I'm sure.

When I'd finally finished, it was lunchtime, and Thomas suggested we go to a Lebanese place down the road.

It was an unpromising little restaurant, with a linoleum floor and plastic tables covered with white paper, but we sat down and ordered.

'I . . . uh,' Thomas said hesitantly, as we waited for our meals. 'I meant what I said the other day. About you staying at my place. I talked about it with Irene, and she said of course.'

The residence shared by Thomas and his girlfriend leapt instantly into my imagination: a rented one-bedroom flat decorated with posters and Fairtrade throw rugs, with potted plants everywhere, a dank bathroom with a cracked sink, a cramped kitchen, and muesli for breakfast. I told myself it was pure prejudice, but I still wasn't remotely tempted. 'That's very kind of you, but I'm sure . . . that is, I don't imagine your place is very big.'

'Well, no. But you could have your own room. We have a sofabed in the lounge: Irene and I could sleep on that.'

'It's very generous of you, but the insurance will cover the hotel, for a week at least. I may go to my mother's after that, if the excitement's died down. I was planning to go there soon anyway, Thomas; she wants time with me. Don't worry about it.'

'I'm sorry about your flat,' he said unhappily. 'I know how I always want to be home when I'm ill; I can't imagine what it feels like to be ill and lose your home. I'm sorry.'

'I've lost things I wanted more,' I told him, thinking of

my hopes for marriage to Ian. 'That's life. It's full of frustration – and then you die. It's not your fault.'

The food arrived – lamb shashlik, paper-thin pita bread with humous, and a salad with cherry tomatoes and chopped onion. It was all freshly prepared and very much better than I'd expected, and I ate with relish.

'I don't know how you do it,' Thomas said admiringly.

'Do what?'

He waved a hand vaguely. 'Keep going. If I had to put up with all the stuff that's been going on with you, I'd be hiding under the bed.'

'I doubt that *very* much! You seemed to cope very well with being arrested as a terrorist!'

'That was an adventure. What's been happening to you is different.'

He meant the cancer. That was thing that preyed upon his mind: that I should be sitting there eating pita bread while Death swelled inside my skull.

'It's not different,' I told him. 'We're *all* going to die – we don't have any choice about it – but, generally speaking, we don't hide under the bed. It'd get boring after a couple of hours, let alone weeks or years. You think being arrested is an adventure?'

'Well, you know. It was like something on television.' He began to smile. 'All these policemen rushing in, in body armour and helmets, with their guns out, and me sitting at the computer like this –' he lifted his hands, eyes widening in astonishment –'wondering what the hell was going on. It wasn't actually the first time I've been arrested, but it was *definitely* the most exciting!'

'It wasn't the first time?'

'Oh, well, it's the sort of thing that happens if you go on enough protests, and I've been on lots. Not violent ones – that is, none of the groups *I've* been with has ever been violent – but sometimes you get arrested anyway, because somebody else is causing trouble, or for obstruction or unlawful assembly or being within a mile of Parliament or whatever. And, uh, well, once I got arrested for criminal damage.'

I gave him a look of mock-alarm and held up my fingers in a vampire-warding cross, and he laughed.

'I poured paint over a bulldozer. It was really stupid. I wouldn't do anything like that now: it just antagonizes people. But I was fourteen at the time, and I was really worked up about this road they were building. There was this bit of woodland, see, where me and my friends used to play when we were little kids. The council put a bypass through the middle of it. I don't know why I thought pouring paint over a bulldozer would help! My parents had to come into court with me and pay a fine and promise that I wouldn't do it again and everything. My dad was furious.'

I smiled at the image of the teenage activist cringing between his parents. 'Have you actually *been* to Malaysia?'

His eyes lit up. 'Oh, yeah! In my gap year I worked in an orangutan sanctuary in Sarawak for a couple of months, and then when I got my degree I went back to Borneo with the Rainforest Trust. It was a volunteer job, at first – I paid my own airfare, and they provided accommodation and food, but no money – but when they saw I knew what I was doing with computers, they hired me to run their website. It's a beautiful country. Very diverse. People think of Islamic countries as all veiled women in black and crazy men with guns, but Malaysia isn't like that at all – it's loud and colourful and exciting. It has *lots* of minorities, and they all live side by side. And, sure, there are problems, but most of the people *like* living in a multicultural society, just like we do in Britain. Crazy mix of technologies, too: everything from Stone Age to cutting-edge electronics. The rainforest, though, that's incredible. You ever seen a rainforest?'

Only in my visions. 'No.'

'It's incredible. The trees are amazing – huge things, with roots that stick out like fans, and the trunks that go up so high it gives you a crick in your neck to look at them. They're dipterocarps, mostly – *keruing,* they call them out there; there are dozens of different sorts. They all fruit at once, and only once every couple of years, so they don't support as much wildlife as the trees in, say, the Amazon. *That's* a forest I'd love to see! But they're fantastic trees. A lot of them have this smell – see, they produce scented resins, balsam and benzoin, to protect themselves against insects and fungus – fungus and mould is a real problem out there, with everything being hot and wet all the time. So when you walk into the forest this *scent* hits you, of wet leaves and decay and resin all mixed up together. You get camphor trees, too – you know camphor, like they used to put in mothballs? I never knew till I got out there that it came from a *tree*. They're not dipterocarps, though, they're laurels; you find them growing here and there in the forest. You can smell them before you see them, sometimes, it's unbelievable! And the flowers! There's one, rafflesia, which is the biggest flower in the world. It's pretty ugly, actually, and it *stinks* – smells like rotting meat – but still, a flower this big –' he extended his hands about a metre apart – 'that's impressive! They're rare now, and endangered, too. I had to walk miles through the forest to see one, but it was worth it when I got there, it really was. And the wildlife you get is fantastic – the orang-utans are so *human*! There's this sense of communication with them that you just don't get with other animals – you can read their expressions and their body language. And the birds are fantastic, too. I could do without the insects, though. Or the land leeches; they make my skin crawl.'

'Leeches?'

'Yeah. See, they live in the leaf mould, on the forest floor, waiting for something warm-blooded to walk by, and when it does, *whup*, they latch on. You wear thick boots and socks up over your trousers, but sometimes they still get you; they crawl up your legs when you're not looking, and you come back to base and find three or four of the things stuck on your side or your back, all swollen up with blood. I hate 'em. The ticks and the mosquitoes are more dangerous – they can carry all sorts of diseases – but it's the leeches that really get to me.'

Leeches had never figured in my hallucinations. I sincerely hoped that didn't change.

'It sounds an amazing place,' I told him.

'It is, it is! People say, "Why bother to preserve the rainforest? It's not a *nice* place; it's dangerous and smelly and full of nasty bugs." And you can say, "It helps regulate the climate and oxygenate the air; you get erosion and desertification if it's destroyed; there are species of plant which have important medicinal properties that haven't even been catalogued and extraordinary animals which have never been studied." And it's all true, but it's not as true as the answer that we should preserve it because it's amazing. Not *nice*, no; not *comfortable*, but amazing. It's like that rafflesia flower: something so different, so extraordinary that it . . . it *enlarges* your ideas about what a flower is, your whole concept of what the universe can contain. If it goes, we can't get it back; we can't *make* something like that, because it's beyond our little comfy middle-class imaginings. It has a value *in itself*, not just because we can *use* it. It shouldn't be destroyed just so a handful of people can make a lot of money out of it!'

I applauded, and he grinned in embarrassment. 'Sorry. I was preaching, wasn't I? But it *is* amazing. You should go— Oh.'

I smiled at him. '"Oh we'll no more, no more to the leafy woods away, to the high wild woods of laurel, and the bowers of bay no more." I wish I could go, but you don't get many wishes in this life. Even in fairy tales you're never offered more than three.'

My phone rang. It was one of my media contacts, shocked, wanting confirmation of the email she'd just read.

Nur Rashidah turned up after lunch and drove me back to the hotel; I told her to keep the car when she'd dropped me off. I don't think she understood that I meant it as a gift, but when I got back to my room I leafed through the pile of documents I'd collected, looking for the registration.

I didn't have it, and remembered that it was in the glove box. I'd have to ask Nur Rashidah – later. I needed to rest.

The phone rang again, however, almost as soon as I'd kicked my shoes off, and I spent most of the afternoon talking on it, telling one reporter after another about the fire, and about my failure to copy Ken's computer disk.

At the end of the fifth call, I realized that I ought to be making phone calls of my own: to the insurers, to the owners of Canalside, to my mother, to the friends I'd arranged to meet that weekend in London. I was too tired, though, and my head felt muzzy with painkillers. I turned my phone off.

I don't know if I fell asleep, but when I opened my eyes,

I was in the rainforest. The huge trunks of the dipterocarps rose all around me, and the green shadow of the leaves filled the sky. I sat up; I was still in my hotel bed, but its pine feet sat in a deep carpet of leafmould. I looked nervously for leeches, but didn't see any. I moved to the centre of the bed anyway. The forest was not real, I knew that, but hallucinatory leeches might be even worse than real ones.

There was a stir at the corner of my eye, and I looked round sharply to see the murdered boy running towards me. He met my eyes beseechingly and pointed wildly at something behind him. I looked, and saw he was pointing at snow, thick white curtains of it. Where it touched the forest the trees were dying.

I turned back to the child – but he was gone, and the trees with him. There was only the hotel bedroom, with my coat over the chair and my shoes scattered across the beige carpet. It was dark outside the window.

The clock on the bedside table said 10:13 in glowing red letters. It had said 3:50 when I last looked at it. I'd missed supper – but when it came down to it, I wasn't hungry.

I got up, cleaned my teeth, took my medications, then went back to bed. I told myself that it didn't mean anything that I was so tired. I'd lost my home; I'd been hospitalized for smoke inhalation; I was taking a couple of powerful drugs. I was entitled to feel very tired. It didn't mean that my condition was getting worse.

I woke next morning still tired. When I switched my phone on, I found a stack of missed calls and voicemails waiting for me.

One of them, I was touched to discover, was Ian wanting to know that I was all right. Another was my mother, still blissfully ignorant of the fire. The rest were journalists.

I dithered over who to answer first – then put the phone away, dressed, and went downstairs to breakfast. If I was to get through the week I would have to pace myself.

After breakfast I dealt with my mother first, taking the most difficult call while I was feeling strongest.

She was, predictably, horrified; also predictable was her declaration that I should come home *at once*. I had to soothe and reassure her. Yes, I was fine, I hadn't even been in the flat when the fire started; I was in the Holiday Inn, the insurance would pay for it for a week; yes, certainly I'd come home, but first I had to see how badly the flat was damaged, and then arrange to sell it.

'Ian was here,' I told her disingenuously. 'We'd arranged that he'd come up on Friday, and he got here a few hours after the fire. He was unbelievably helpful.'

As I'd expected, this distracted her into a commentary on how wonderful it was, and I was able to get away without setting a precise date to come home.

Ian's phone was busy. I sent him a text. *I'm ok; maybe see you at mum's.* I also texted the friends I'd been supposed to meet in London. It had been arranged for the following weekend, and I was already certain that I wouldn't be able to manage it.

The journalists took up more time. One of the messages turned out to be from *Panorama*, which was looking at the possibility of a programme on illegal logging. They asked if they could record a segment with me at once, 'as a test' (i.e., they knew that if they left it until they'd made up their minds whether or not to do the programme, I'd be permanently unavailable.) I agreed, as I agreed to the three other interviews; I also referred all of them to Thomas Holden and the Rainforest Trust. I had a rest for a bit, then set to work on the insurers and Canalside.

When I prepared for bed that night, I was satisfied that I'd managed to get quite a lot done. When I lay down, though, it struck me that I hadn't left the hotel all day. If I didn't stop feeling so tired, the interviews I'd agreed to would be difficult.

They were. I had the three print media on Wednesday, and the *Panorama* segment on Thursday. We used the hotel conference room. Thomas came and joined me on Wednesday afternoon and all of Thursday. The television people took hours – they weren't sure what the thrust of the proposed programme was going to be, so they had to ask about everything.

They liked Thomas, though. When they were finally packing the cameras away, they asked him if he'd be willing to go out to Malaysia with a crew, to introduce his Rainforest partners. He agreed enthusiastically.

When *Panorama* at last left, I was so tired I didn't even want to walk up to my room. I sat down in one of the conference room chairs and rested my head on the table. Thomas helped me up and took me to my room.

'Thanks,' I told him muzzily, lying down on the bed.

'Can I do anything?'

I let him fetch me my medications and a glass of water. 'Are you going to be all right?' he asked, when I'd downed the pills. His anxiety told me I didn't look it.

'I'll be OK when I've had a rest.' I managed a weak smile. 'The painkillers I'm taking make me feel tired all the time. Don't worry. The worst is over: the media will now lose interest in us. By next week, they'll have forgotten us completely. I'll probably go home to my mother's after the weekend.'

'Don't leave without saying goodbye,' he told me seriously. 'I'd really hate it if you did that.'

'We can have a goodbye supper, then,' I suggested. 'Let Nur Rashidah cook her Malaysian meal.'

'That would be good,' he said, and smiled.

Rosewood
Dalbergia nigra
Brazil

On the Red list as 'vulnerable'; on the CITES appendix banning trade in endangered species

Eleven

We arranged to have a farewell supper on Sunday evening. I phoned my mother again, and we agreed that she would collect me on Monday. I wasn't sure that I could finish sorting out the sale of the flat or the insurance by then, but I was doing those by telephone anyway, and I was beginning to long for a place I could call home. As Thomas had said, being ill on my own in a hotel was no fun. I'd done what the police advised, and I felt reasonably confident that nobody would chase after me to make my life hell.

I didn't read the papers on Thursday; I was too exhausted. I gathered, though, that Masterpiece Home Design was very unhappy about the coverage, because Colin Douglas of Griffin Legal phoned me first thing Friday morning.

'How did you get this number?' I asked him, then realized that, of course, the company had always had the number of my mobile.

'Our clients,' he duly replied. 'Ms Lanchester, I had some sympathy for you, but you've gone too far! Our clients are taking out a writ against you.'

I sighed and rubbed my aching eyes. 'Why? It's a waste of everyone's time and energy: you have to know that.'

'This latest allegation *cannot* be allowed to stand unchallenged! My clients are not arsonists!'

I was taken aback. 'I never said they were! In fact, I *said* I didn't think they were responsible!'

There was a silence. 'You did?'

'Oh, God! Look, I don't even know what the papers have said about it: I haven't read any since the weekend. I certainly *tried* to make it clear that I blame whoever it was that dear old Ken Norman was blackmailing, but it's hard to do that

when I can't say straight out that he's suspected of blackmail – which I can't, since it's still under investigation. I'm
very tired and I'm ill and maybe I wasn't as coherent as I
should've been. If you like, I'll provide you with a signed
statement saying that I do not blame Masterpiece Home
Design for the fire, and your precious clients can wave it at
the newspapers to their hearts' content.'

There was another silence, this one bewildered. 'Mr
Norman is suspected of blackmail?'

'Haven't you talked to the police?'

'No. Of course not! This is a *civil* case, not a *criminal*
one!'

'Didn't you even *wonder* about it? I mean, you must have
wanted to talk to my boss about what I took from his
computer. I would've thought that when he turned up dead,
you'd at least *ask* about it!'

'But . . . he committed suicide! Didn't he?'

'Oh, Lord!' He didn't know *anything*, except what his
clients had chosen to tell him.

'He didn't?' Douglas asked, now with nervous fascination.

I hesitated. 'Look, I don't know any of the details, and,
as I said, the whole thing is still under investigation – but I
do know that the police were calling it a homicide. They
suspect Ken had information he shouldn't have had, and that
he was using it to blackmail somebody, or possibly several
somebodies. Nobody knows more than that – but the police
told me that the fire was probably intended to destroy
evidence which somebody believed *I* had. They advised me
to make it clear that I never had anything beyond the three
documents I handed over to the Rainforest Trust. That was
what I was trying to do earlier this week, and I'm sorry if
it came out wrong.'

'Oh. *Oh.* I, uh, I didn't know any of that.'

'No, I can see that. Do you want me to provide a statement saying I don't blame the company?'

'Oh. Yes. Thank you. Um. I should come round and collect
that. Could I do it this afternoon?'

I arranged to meet him in the lobby of the hotel at two p.m.
I was sitting with a coffee and a newspaper when he came

in – I guessed immediately who it was, though we'd never met. He matched my mental image very neatly: a plump, prissy man of about thirty in a good suit, carrying a brief-case. I set my newspaper down.

When I looked up again, though, there was snow everywhere – not a blizzard this time, but a thick dense carpet underfoot. Above me the hotel's low ceiling had become a heavy sky, cheer-less with winter. I sat in my leather-upholstered hotel-lobby chair, shocked and disturbed, as Colin Douglas walked through the snow towards me. There was another man with him, tall and white-haired, also dressed in a good suit. His face was familiar, but I couldn't remember his name or where I'd met him.

'Mrs Lanchester?' Douglas asked, bending over and extending a pink hand.

I took the hand and shook it, trying not to stare at the icy wilderness all around us.

'Antonia Lanchester,' said the other man, scowling. He did not offer his hand.

Douglas smiled and sat down opposite me, the seat seem-ingly appearing out of icy wilderness as his buttocks descended into it. When he had seated himself, the other man abruptly sat down as well. He watched me with bitter resentment.

'I've drafted a statement for you,' Douglas said, opening the briefcase and taking out a sheet of paper. 'If you could just sign it *there*, we'll be able to sort out the misunder-standing with the press.'

'Let me read it first.'

The statement doubled in my distorted vision, and I had to pinch the bridge of my nose and shut my eyes for a moment. When I opened them again I could make it out. *I do not hold Masterpiece Home Design responsible for the harrassment I have suffered . . . I acknowledge that they have conducted themselves lawfully at all times . . .*

'No,' I said, handing it back. 'It's too strong. If you show that to the media they'll think MHD had *nothing* to do with what's been happening to me – that the harrass-ment was from an ex-boyfriend or something. If you give me paper and a pen, Mr Douglas, I'll write a statement of my own.'

'But you said you accepted my clients weren't responsible for harrassing—' began Douglas.

'I never said any such thing. I *also* consider it harrassment to threaten a law suit.'

'That was perfectly legal!' snapped the older man. 'You
clearly stole property and breached our trust!'

I raised my eyebrows. 'I'm not contesting that, or your right
to sue, but making the law suit contingent on my "coopera-
tion" in "clearing your name", *that* is harrassment, in my view.'

'We haven't broken any laws!'

'I don't think I've ever said you did. Other people broke
laws: all you did was profit from it. If you really think
there's nothing wrong with that, why are you so upset that
I exposed it?'

He glared. 'I've been building up this company for the
last ten years! Ten years of *hard work*! We were providing
a quality product to customers who were happy to get it –
ordinary people who liked having something beautiful and
extraordinary in their homes – and we were providing jobs
in this country, turning an honest profit, and paying our taxes.
I've always been proud of this company, and suddenly we're
monsters, and I'm being treated like a, a *child molester*!'
Snow fell in powdery clumps from the arm of his chair as
his hands fisted.

'Alfred Howarth,' I said, finally remembering his name.
He was CEO of Masterpiece Home Design; his photo had
smiled at me from the company literature for three years.

'Oh!' said Douglas nervously. 'I thought you'd met before.'

Howarth gave me a look of distaste. 'Ms Lanchester never
came to my attention *before*.'

Snow was beginning to sift down from the close white
sky. I tried not to look, to watch the faces of the men before
me. 'You could make beautiful and extraordinary furniture
with *certified* hardwoods.'

He made a noise of disgust. 'Why shouldn't we use timber
which the exporting countries are perfectly happy to sell to
us? And why shouldn't countries which have natural resources
make the most of them? Why should *we* tell them what to
do, or police their laws for them?'

'Because people in this country want to buy a product that

I do not hold Masterpiece Home Design corporately
responsible for the fire which destroyed my home. The
police have informed me that it was probably the work
of private individuals who had some connection to the
documents I leaked.

I set the pen down and pinched my nose again. 'Sorry. My
eyes are bad this morning. The tumour is compressing them
at the back. I'm not sure how to phrase the rest, either.' I
lowered my hand and met Alfred Howarth's eyes mildly. 'Mr
Howarth, would you like to draft your version of what I
should say? I'm willing to let you do that, as a sign of how
much I regret the way the media's taken this. It just needs
to say that I accept that you haven't done anything illegal.
I'll look it over when I've rested my eyes a moment.'

He grunted, glanced at Douglas, then took a sheet of paper.
I sat back in the chair and closed my eyes.

When I opened them again, I found, to my great relief,
that the snow had vanished. I took the page Howarth was
offering and squinted at the line of spiky handwriting.

'I'm sorry, I can't read it. It's my eyes, like I said. Could
you print it?'

He snarled, but copied over what he'd written. I took the
sheet, thanked him, and glanced over it. *I acknowledge that
Masterpiece Home Design has broken no laws and is
not responsible for any of the illegal harrassment I've
experienced.*

'I'll accept that,' I agreed, and carefully added the sentence
to my own statement, adding only the word 'corporately'
before 'responsible'. I signed and dated the statement and
handed it to Colin Douglas. 'If you want to refer the press
back to me, I'm willing to confirm,' I told him. 'But you
should warn them that I'm going home to stay with family
on Monday. My mobile number will still work, though, and
I hope to get my email going again if anybody needs to
contact me.'

Douglas thanked me and got to his feet. Howarth rose too,
scowling. I pinched my nose and shut my eyes again, to
excuse myself from getting up, and I didn't see them leave.

When they were gone, I picked up the sheet of paper on

which Howarth had printed his disclaimer. I couldn't remember now exactly what the threatening note had looked like – but O'Connor and Summers presumably still had it. They might be interested in Howarth's visit, and they could compare the handwriting.

On Saturday morning Nur Rashidah took me on a brief excursion, to pick up a few small items and to drop off a form at the central post office to redirect my mail. We stopped by Canalside on the way back, to collect all the post that had come since the fire.

There was a lot of it: my letterbox had overflowed, and the stack on the floor beneath it was so tall that items were falling off and getting kicked into corners. Most of it seemed to be cards, and when I tore one open I saw that it was from a complete stranger.

> I saw your interview in the paper, and I was so moved. If you can fight for the planet when you're battling cancer, the rest of us can surely do it when we're healthy. God bless you! I opened another. I just wanted to express my deep admiration for what you're doing. You're so brave. Don't let the bastards get to you.

I showed them to Nur Rashidah, and she beamed. 'People have seen what you are doing,' she told me. 'How you are fighting for the good of the world, even though you are so ill. Are you surprised that they want to thank you?'

She carefully collected all the stray cards, then put my stack of post in with my shopping and carried it all back to the car. I took everything back to the hotel to examine at leisure.

It wasn't all messages of support. There was a letter from the hospital, telling me I should go in for an appointment on 'palliative care', which reminded me that I would have to notify them that I was moving. There were leaflets from victim-support services; there were *three* thick A4 envelopes of forms from the insurers – and, to my deep relief, there was a cheque from my private pension scheme, the proceeds of cashing in. It amounted to some eight thousand pounds – not as much as I'd hoped, but more than enough to carry me over any temporary problems with, say, hotel bills.

I tucked the cheque into my purse and began opening the cards. There were a few from friends and acquaintances, but most were from strangers – over a hundred of them. They'd seen my story in the papers and wanted to express their sympathy and support. *You're so brave*, they said, again and again, and *I'm so glad you stood up for the planet.* Some of them, to my embarrassment, included money *to help you get back on your feet* or *for the rainforest.*

I'd always said I detested this sort of ignorant public slush of emotion, this assumption that you were familiar with someone because you'd seen a carefully crafted presentation in the media. I didn't detest this at all, though. I was moved to tears. I felt that yes, I had been brave, I had accomplished something worthwhile. I had to forcibly remind myself that I hadn't *set out* to be a noble martyr of the environmental movement: I'd set out to fire a parting shot at my detestable employers.

About two thirds of the way through the stack I had to stop: I was overwhelmed. I knew, too, that somebody was going to have to reply to all of these – or, at least, to thank the people who'd sent money. I supposed I could turn the task, and the money, over to the Rainforest Trust.

As I was putting the cards aside on the dresser, I noticed a letter. I picked it up because it was different from the others, and I lay down on the bed.

Dear Antonia Lanchester,
Probly you dont want to hear from me, but I had to write to say how sorry I am. The police have been telling me all the horrible things that Ken was doing, and I feel so bad about it. Going after a woman with brain cancer like that, thats just sick. I'm so sorry. And now I hear that youve lost your home, too. Please let me know if theres anything I can do to make up for it. I dont have a lot of money right now, but they say Katie will get Ken's stuff, so we could help out if you need anything.
Yours,
Elsie Norman (Ken's ex-wife)

I was touched. There was a phone number, so I dialled it.

The voice that answered was too young: a girl not yet out of her teens. 'Hiya!'

'May I speak to Elsie Norman?'

'Oh, right. *Mu-um!* It's for you!'

A pause; the clunk of a phone being set down and picked up again. 'Hello?'

'Mrs Norman? This is Antonia Lanchester. I just got your letter.'

'Oh!' This was said with alarm. 'Oh, I hope I didn't offend you. I just felt so bad about—'

'No, no! I was very touched, and I wanted to thank you. I don't need any help, but it was very kind of you to offer it.'

'Oh,' Relieved this time. 'Oh, that's good of you. I just had to say how sorry I was. I mean, Ken was no angel, but the sort of things the police have been saying the last few days, I was *horrified*.'

'I was very impressed that you thought about me at all. To tell the truth, I've, uh, felt bad for you and for your daughter ever since I heard you were the ones who found the body.'

'Oh, that's so kind of you. It *was* a terrible shock. I was very worried about Katie afterwards. But she seems to be getting over it, thanks very much.'

'How old is she?'

'Thirteen. A lovely girl. She normally stays – *stayed* – with her dad two weekends a month, and I drove her over there on Saturday morning. Last time I almost drove away soon as I dropped her off, but thank God, I waited to be sure everything was all right. It makes me sick to think she could have been left all on her own with what was inside that house! See, sometimes Ken would forget she was coming, and then he'd go out and leave the house locked up. It wasn't locked then, but I waited just in case – and then she came running out, white as a sheet and crying. She was that upset she couldn't even tell me what was wrong! I went back in with her, and it was *terrible*. I don't know how we got through the rest of the day.'

'It must've been dreadful.'

'Oh, *terrible*! He was shot three times, the police said, and there was just blood everywhere. I didn't recognize him – only his hands; I knew it was him when I saw his hands. I wish to God Katie hadn't seen it, it was a nightmare! And I was thinking, how on earth could something like this happen to Ken? And then the police said that he was probably blackmailing somebody, and that the person he was blackmailing must've turned on him after you gave those letters to that rainforest charity. They said he'd broken into your house and wrecked it, and taken your computer and your credit cards and all. I was so ashamed!'

'None of it was your fault.'

'I know, but still. He was my husband. I'm sorry, I talk too much. Ken always said I had a mouth like a drainpipe, everything just pours out! I should be asking about you. I felt just awful when I read about it in the papers, how you lost your house and everything, when you're so ill. You sure you don't need help?'

'I'm fine. I was going home to stay with my mother anyway, and the insurance will pay for most of what I lost. I was really just phoning to thank you for your concern.'

'Oh, well! My Katie, she thinks it's great, what you're doing. She's very into animals and the environment. You can never leave a light on in this house without she tells you off, and she's always after me to buy organic. You know, she *knew* about this business of logging rainforests, before you made all this noise about it in the papers? She had an argument with her dad about it only a couple of months ago! He has this table he bought for the sitting room. It's rosewood – not from roses like we have, but from some tree in South America – and he told her she couldn't do her homework on it because it was very rare and valuable. Katie told him right out he should be ashamed of killing a rare tree to make furniture! She speaks her mind, my Katie.'

'Good for her!'

'Yes,' agreed Elsie Norman proudly. 'She's a clever girl. I never did like that Alfred Howarth that wrote those letters you stole.'

'You knew him?'

'Oh, yes. Ken said they used to go mountain climbing

together when they were students. He gave Ken his job, and they'd meet up sometimes, you know, in the pub. I used to tell Ken he ought to invite him and Isobel Howarth round to dinner, but he never did. I think he was ashamed to, actually, because I'm not very good at fancy dinners. He hardly ever invited people round.'

'I don't think he was very good with people.'

'No. He never was, and he got worse. Things would go wrong, and he'd lose his temper. People go wrong, don't they? Without even meaning to.'

I thought of the way my own life had twisted away from me. 'That's true.'

'I loved him,' Elsie Norman said sadly, 'but I'm ashamed of what he did, that's the truth.'

I imagined their marriage: Ken bullying and belittling her. Everything about her speech proclaimed her as working class, poorly educated, and lacking in confidence. He'd probably married her because she was easy to dominate. She, however, was the one with the 'lovely daughter' and a life ahead of her; he was in his grave. 'It doesn't seem to me that *you* need to be ashamed of anything,' I told her warmly.

When we'd ended the call, with expressions of goodwill on both sides, I thought about what she'd said. Ken and Alfred Howarth had been students together? That didn't make sense: there had been too many years between them. True, I wasn't sure of the exact age of either man, but Howarth looked to be sixtyish, while Ken couldn't have been more than ten years older than I was myself. I supposed that Howarth *could* have gone back to university for a second degree while Ken was an undergraduate, but it still seemed unlikely that they would have had much to do with one another. Mature graduate students certainly hadn't mixed with undergraduates at my university.

Maybe it *could* happen, though, in particular societies where a small group of enthusiasts got together. Elsie Norman had said they went *mountain climbing* together.

I imagined the two much younger, setting off on a mountain-climbing expedition together, looking up eagerly at the pure peaks ahead of them. I thought of the pictures on Ken's computer, and there was a prickle along my skin, as there had been the night when I first looked at them – a sense of something horrible buried. I wondered if it was yet another creation of my oppressed brain or a real intuition.

Should I telephone O'Connor? No. My suspicion was too tenuous. Besides, I was sure he and Summers had interviewed Elsie Norman repeatedly, and if they hadn't already asked her about Howarth, they certainly would now that I'd drawn their attention to him.

Nur Rashidah collected me for the farewell supper at about five o'clock on Sunday afternoon – the early hour was because she didn't want to abandon her cooking after she'd started it.

Elm Tree, the international students' residence, was a rather drab pebbledash block, three stories high, enclosed in beds of laurel. Nur Rashidah parked the Porsche in a slot at the back of the building and escorted me inside.

Her room was on the second floor. It was, I suppose, bigger than that of most undergraduates, but it was still small: bed, desk, bookshelf laden with microbiology texts, one armchair. I didn't see how she was going to fit everyone in for the dinner.

'There is a common room,' she told me, noticing my doubtful look. 'I have told the others on this corridor that I will be using it this evening. There is no problem. They eat by themselves in their own rooms anyway.' There was a world of dismay at the coldness of her neighbours contained in that last quiet statement.

'Where's the kitchen?'

'It is down the corridor. But you should rest for a little while, Toni. I know the last week has been very hard for you.'

'I can chop onions or something.'

I was not allowed to chop onions, but I was allowed to sit on a folding chair watching Nur Rashidah do so. She chopped them with a frowning concentration which hinted that she hadn't actually done so very often. I wondered how she'd fed herself since arriving in Britain. Sandwiches? Pot noodles?

'Do you have much of your degree left to do?' I asked.

'Only this last year. I will go home in the summer.'

'You must be looking forward to that.'

She gave me a warm smile. 'My first year I was, oh, *so* wanting to go home! This year it is not so bad. I have friends now – you, and Thomas, and the people in the university Islamic Society.'

She told me about her friends in the Islamic Society as she continued to prepare the meal. It appeared they normally met for Friday prayers and a meal; occasionally they had a speaker on topics ranging from Art to Ethics. Meanwhile, the onions were joined by green chillis, garlic, ginger, and lemongrass. The kitchen began to fill with the scents of southern Asia, and I started to feel hungry for the first time in several days.

'My religion is a great joy to me,' Nur Rashidah went on shyly. 'When I am sad and the world seems ugly, I know that the ugliness is only small, and beyond it there is the infinite beauty of God. That gives me peace.'

She'd exercised great restraint in not trying to convert me before this, so I took care with my answer. 'I'm sure religion is a great comfort to believers.'

'And you do not believe? Not at all?'

I considered that seriously. 'I wouldn't say that. It's just that people say lots of different things about God and the afterlife, and the truth is something we cannot *know* in this world. There's no test we can do to see who's right – except the test of seeing for ourselves, and then we can't report back.'

'We can trust, without knowing. We must do that, or what are our lives? We must trust our parents, our friends, our doctors, even our *banks*. Why should it be so much more to trust the messengers of God?'

'I'm sorry, Nur Rashidah, but when I look at the world, what I see doesn't incline me to trust in a beneficient Creator.'

She was silent a moment, frowning as she stirred her sauce. 'For me, when I look at the natural world I see beauty and wonder. Evil is human.'

'Earthquakes,' I responded. 'Floods. Disease.' I hesitated, then added, 'Astrocytomas.'

She didn't flinch at that, just turned and fixed me with her earnest gaze. 'We cannot understand the will of God. We can only submit, and trust. For me, I cannot believe that goodness and beauty are nothing, that we make them with our own minds. They are there, surely, in the world outside us – and if they are real, then they are precious, surely! We must trust that they are *more* than all the world's evils, and that the God who gave them deserves our trust and our love.'

'Where does evil come from? I understand what you're saying, but I don't think you can prove any theory about things *outside* this world while we are, in fact, confined to it. Belief, faith – it's an act of will, a deliberate decision to commit yourself beyond what can be known. If God damns people because they won't trust what they don't know and can't prove, then I'm damned. Sorry.'

She shook her head. 'I trust that God's compassion is greater than ours, not less.'

'I'll find out soon,' I told her, smiling, trying to lighten the air.

She did not smile back, merely nodded.

Thomas and his girlfriend turned up at about seven with a box of chocolates; Rafi about twenty minutes later. Nur Rashidah made tea – as a good Muslim, of course, she wouldn't serve alcohol – and we drank it in the 'common room'. This was a rather cheerless place with green carpet tiles and chrome chairs upholstered in black vinyl, but we succeeded in ignoring the surroundings.

I'd brought along all the cards with money in them – the total came to a hundred and eighty-five pounds. I'd endorsed all the cheques, and I handed the lot over to Thomas in a plastic bag, for safety, with the cheques tucked inside the relevant cards for ease in replying.

'I don't need the money,' I explained, 'and half of them are "for the rainforest" anyway. Somebody should reply and thank the donors and, to tell the truth, I don't think I'm up to it.' My eyes were still bothering me.

Thomas accepted the money with enthusiasm. 'This is great! One of our partners needs money for a land survey: this will get them started!'

'You don't mean to use it in your office?'

He dismissed the office's charity shop and back-street poverty with a decisive wave. 'We're *fine* already. The place they really *need* money is out in the field. Can I have your mother's address, in case we get any more cards for you?'

I gave everyone my mother's address and my email, wrote theirs in my appointments diary, and we all promised to keep in touch.

Nur Rashidah's party piece was chicken in a coconut sauce, served with rice; it was very good. We all ate too much and, when we could manage no more, she put the remains in a tupperware dish and made coffee. We sat about, replete, sipping, nibbling from the box of chocolates.

'Here's to our hero!' Thomas said, toasting me with his coffee cup. 'You've done more for the rainforest in the past four weeks than I've managed in my lifetime!'

'I doubt that,' I said, but they all toasted me, smiling, and I felt warm and triumphant. I looked round the circle of my friends – and saw the murdered child, standing silently between Thomas and Nur Rashidah. His face was solemn.

'What is the matter?' asked Nur Rashidah, glancing round to see what I was staring at. I thought for a moment that she must see him too – but, of course, she didn't. I reminded myself that he wasn't real.

'Nothing,' I told her, forcing myself to look aside. 'Just tired.'

'You should rest,' she replied at once.

'A moment.' I dug in my handbag, found the registration of the Porsche, which I'd filled in for a change of ownership. I handed it to Nur Rashidah. She was shocked, and tried to refuse, but I insisted. At last she took it, looking distressed. The child had vanished again, to my relief.

I gave Rafi and Thomas each a cheque 'to buy a Christmas present', and apologized because I hadn't had time to shop for them. They thanked me and wrung my hand, all of them now close to tears.

'You're welcome to sell the car,' I advised Nur Rashidah. 'You can use the money any way you choose.'

'I would like it better if you could use it,' she told me, then took her specs off and wiped her eyes.

'I would, too, if it comes to that,' I said, again trying for a light tone. 'But you don't always get what you want. Come on, take me home.'

Eaglewood
Aquilaria malaccensis
Southern Asia

Listed as 'vulnerable' on the Red list; critically
endangered in India; on the CITES appendix
banning trade in endangered species

doesn't involve violence and the destruction of an irre-placeable natural resource. Why are you here, Mr Howarth? Just to relieve your feelings by telling me how wicked I've been to damage an honest, hard-working company?'

He made a face. 'You told Mr Douglas that the police suspect that Kenneth Norman was engaged in blackmail.'

Had he not heard that before? Or did he want to compare notes? 'That's what they told me. They said that the arson attack on my flat was probably to destroy evidence, and they advised me to make it clear that I don't have any. I'm sorry that my attempt to do that led some of the media to imply that Masterpiece Home Design are arsonists. I never intended that, and I'm willing to set the record straight.'

He grunted. 'So I'm to understand that you don't have any more little bombshells waiting to drop on us? Mr Norman told me that you'd copied the documents folder off his computer.'

'He was wrong. All I did was print out three items, and I gave all of them to the Rainforest Trust the very next day. It didn't occur to me to copy his hard disk: I'm just not a computer person.'

Another grunt; a moment of silence. 'Who do they think he was blackmailing?'

'They really don't know. My guess would be some govern-ment minister in Malaysia – but that's just a guess.' Even as I said it, I wondered. His presence, and his questions, seemed to be concerned with something other than the well-being of the company. And he'd brought the snow . . .

. . . Which was a hallucination, the product of my own tormented brain, and no reason at all to suspect him. Even if my subconscious was trying to show me something, it had no hotline to the Ultimate Truth.

'I'm willing to write out a statement saying that I don't hold MHD responsible for arson or for any *illegal* harrass-ment,' I offered.

Howarth made a noise of anger and impatience, but Douglas agreed at once. He took a blank sheet of paper from his briefcase and offered me his pen.

I squinted at it, then wrote:

Twelve

The whole farewell party accompanied me down to the car and stood about in the chilly dark for rather longer than I wanted, talking and well-wishing and hugging. When I was finally allowed to climb into the Porsche, Thomas suddenly remembered the money I'd handed him, and decided that it was essential that it be locked in the office safe at once.

'Do you suppose you could just give me a lift by the office?' he asked hopefully. 'It would only take a minute. I can come back here and collect my bike afterwards.'

We didn't really have any choice except to agree. Irene kissed Thomas goodnight and mounted her bicycle; Rafi waved and climbed into his Toyota. Thomas slid into the back seat of the Porsche, clutching the plastic bag of greeting cards containing money. Nur Rashidah drove us cautiously out into the darkness.

It was late enough that the shops near the Rainforest Trust were closed, and Nur Rashidah was able to park immediately outside the door. Thomas jumped out of the car and went up to the shop door, key in hand; I saw him hesitate just before he reached it, but he unlocked the door and went in.

Nur Rashidah and I sat in the car in silence, waiting. I was watching the door, which was ajar, when the murdered child slid through it.

He was half-naked and barefoot, as always, and untroubled by the cold November night, but he seemed otherwise as real and as solid as Thomas had, standing at the same door a minute before. He looked directly into my face, then glanced over his shoulder and went back inside.

I let my breath out in a silent gasp and opened the passenger door.

'What is the matter?' asked Nur Rashidah in surprise.

'I think something's wrong.' The child wasn't real – I *knew* he wasn't real – but he represented something true and important. I couldn't possibly just continue to sit quietly in the car. Perhaps my subconscious had picked up on something my conscious mind had missed; perhaps I was just nervous, but I had to go and check.

I went into the dingy charity shop, with Nur Rashidah following close behind me. It was dark, but there was a light in the office beyond it – light, and a cry of alarm.

'No!' exclaimed Thomas, his voice high-pitched with fear. 'Don't, please! You don't have to do this!'

There was a reply, low, inaudible. I dug my fingers into my palm, wondering if I had time to phone the police – then flung open the door to the office.

Thomas was standing a couple of paces in front of me, his hands in the air; facing him across the desk was a man in dark clothing, his face covered with a black balaclava. Despite the balaclava, I had no difficulty recognizing Alfred Howarth. He had a gun in his hand, and it was pointed at Thomas, angled to catch him in the chest.

'Mr Howarth,' I said evenly. 'Please put down the gun.'

Howarth's jaw dropped, making his mouth a hole in the black wool that concealed his face. The gun moved up, then wavered. The walls of the room vanished, and suddenly we were standing in the forest, in the green dusk of innumerable leaves. The murdered boy was standing at the foot of one of the great dipterocarps, a slim brown hand resting on its great buttress root, watching us with a solemn face.

'There's no point in shooting anybody,' I told Howarth quietly. 'The police are already on their way, and they already suspect you. Killing us now won't save you: it will only make your situation even worse. Please put the gun down.'

'You phoned the police?' asked Howarth, voice rising in alarm.

'Before we came in,' I agreed. 'They're on their way.'

'Shit!' He glanced around wildly, his movements jerky with fear. Thomas took a hasty step back and caught my arm. I wasn't sure whether he was intending to thrust me out of the line of fire or just clinging to me like a frightened child: perhaps it was both.

'Mr Howarth,' I said, very gently, 'you can't make this go away, whatever you do now. You *can* still manage it, though. You're a rich man, you can hire good lawyers and get off lightly – provided you stop *now*.'

'You bitch!' breathed Howarth, in a voice so low I barely caught the word. 'I've got nothing to lose: I've already committed *murder*!'

'You can claim provocation. Ken was blackmailing you for years, wasn't he? You can make a case for manslaughter: you went over there to discuss the situation and there was a quarrel. You defended yourself; the gun went off in the struggle . . . A good lawyer could ensure you came out of prison in only a couple of years, with time off for good behaviour. If you kill Thomas, though – or me – it will be murder; or even *double* murder, in cold blood. You're not stupid: I know you can see how much worse it would be.'

'I'm not going to prison!'

'A couple of years, Mr Howarth. In an open prison, probably. You could catch up on your reading, take up a new hobby. Then you'd be out. You'd still have your family, your pension, your holidays in the sun. Is that worth nothing to you? I wish I had as much! But if you keep on making this worse, you'll be *sent* somewhere worse, and you'll stay there very much longer. You know that what I'm saying is true.'

'Just give me the disk!' His voice was rising. 'Just let me get rid of that!'

'There was *no* disk. I told you that.'

'You were *lying*! You think I couldn't see that you were lying? You even *told* me that the police told you to say it! *Ken* said there was a disk!'

'He was *wrong*. There never was a computer disk. Whatever you did up on that mountain all those years ago, it's buried where no one will ever find it.'

Howarth jumped, and the gun went off, its percussion deafening, bewildering me with the echoes of a confined space when my eyes told me that we were in a wilderness. I didn't – couldn't – see where the bullet had gone, but beside me Thomas seemed unharmed, and nobody was screaming. I took two quick steps forward and Howarth turned the gun back on me with the jerky speed of a jack-in-the-box erupting. The black muzzle confronted me.

I raised both hands. Beyond Howarth, the little boy took a step forward, his face full of anxiety.

'There was no disk,' I said, keeping my voice level, unexcited. 'Your secret is safe.'

'How do you know about it, then?' asked Howarth, suddenly loud and furious. 'If it's secret, how do you *know* what happened on the mountain?'

'I *don't* know. All I know is that you and Ken met climbing mountains, and that he had a hold on you afterwards. I was *guessing* that something happened. If you say I'm wrong, I can't challenge you on it. There is nothing that anyone could produce in court; *nothing*.'

He stood transfixed, breathing hard. 'I don't believe you.'

I took another step forward. I wasn't frightened at all. I felt astonishingly calm, even happy. 'I'm going to die soon, whatever happens, so if you shoot me, I don't lose much. The loss would be to you, in the sentence you'd get for my murder. I'm going to take away that gun before you do any more harm with it.'

'No!' he choked. He took a step back, but could not take a second one: his back was against the bole of one of the great trees.

I took another step forward, then another. I put my hand out and closed it on the barrel of the gun. It was hot under my palm as I drew it out of Howarth's unresisting grasp. He slumped against the tree, then slid down it slowly and buried his face in his hands, the balaclava peeling away into a black ruff over his hair.

The murdered boy smiled at me and came over, stretching out his little hand to take the gun. The rainforest vanished, and everything went dark.

The next thing I was aware of was a splitting pain in my head and a feeling that I'd been knocked down and trampled. Somebody was wiping my face with something cool. I opened my eyes and saw Nur Rashidah's anxious face hanging over me. For the first time since I met her, she was not wearing her scarf. She looked younger without it, her face childishly soft. A few tendrils of black hair curled against her cheeks; the rest was tucked in a thick wave behind her ears.

My eyes met hers, and the gentle strokes of the cloth stopped. 'Toni?'

'Mm.' I tried to look round without moving my head. I was in Thomas Holden's office, lying on the floor, my head in Nur Rashidah's lap. There were other people in the room, but from my position on the floor I couldn't really see them. I felt too ill even to be curious about who they were.

'It's all right,' she told me, catching and squeezing my hand. 'Nobody is hurt. The ambulance will be here soon.'

'Police,' I muttered, remembering my lie.

'They are coming, too.'

'What happened? Somebody hit me?'

She wiped my brow again, and I realized that the cloth she was using was her scarf, dipped in water. 'I think you had some kind of seizure. He gave you the gun, and then you fell down in convulsions. It is all right: nobody is hurt. Thomas is looking after the gun.'

The ambulance arrived before the police: I was being helped into it when the squad car pulled up, lights flashing, to take charge of Alfred Howarth. I was still very muzzy-headed, and it was some time before it occurred to me that he could easily have run off when I collapsed. He hadn't; he'd surrendered and cooperated. I suppose he'd already stopped trying to make his problem go away, and had started trying to manage it.

Nur Rashidah came into the hospital with me, sat with me while I waited for attention, fetched drinks of water and blankets, and answered questions I was too stunned to remember how to answer. When I woke in the morning, it was to find her slumped asleep in a chair beside my hospital bed. She had taken off her specs, but put the scarf on again at some point during the night. It had slipped down over one eye, giving her a comical look, like a child in a too-large hat. I watched her in silence for several minutes.

A nurse came in with a battery of monitoring equipment,

and Nur Rashidah sat up groggily. She saw that I was awake and gave me a weary smile as she fumbled for her specs on the bedside table.

'Now, Toni,' said the nurse cheerily, 'we just need to check your blood pressure and your heart . . .'

I submitted to the checks. 'What happened to me?'

The nurse's smile fixed momentarily. 'We'll do some more tests this morning, but it sounds as though you had a seizure. You're one of Dr Hillman's patients, are you?'

'Yes. Terminal brain cancer.'

The smile vanished, replaced by an expression of commiserating concern. 'Yes. I'm very sorry. I'm afraid that seizures are a very common feature of the disease as it progresses. We'll do some tests this morning, and then the doctor will give you some medication to help control it.'

More medications. I knew, with absolute conviction, that I was on my way now. I had had one last month of real life. What lay ahead was increasing disability and pain, and stronger and stronger drugs to 'control' them. Death, when it came, would be a release.

I hoped I made it through Christmas. It would be good to have one last Christmas with my family, and leave quietly with the new year.

'I was supposed to go home this afternoon,' I objected. 'My mother was coming to pick me up.'

'It would be better if she could wait till tomorrow.'

Behind the nurse, the wall vanished, turning to trees. The light rippled, green and warm. I looked for the child, but he wasn't there – not yet. He would come back, I was sure of it.

'Toni?' asked Nur Rashidah softly.

I tore my eyes away. 'Where's my phone?'

'I'm afraid you're not allowed to use mobile phones in the hospital,' said the nurse.

There was a noise from among the trees – from the corridor, I suppose – and then Thomas came in, closely followed by Detectives Summers and O'Connor. Thomas came straight to the bed and put his arms around me – awkwardly, because I was lying back against the pillow, but with deep feeling. 'Oh, Toni!' he said thickly. 'I thought you were going to die. You saved my life!'

'Who's the brave heroine?' asked O'Connor. 'Ah, nurse!' He dug out his ID and showed it to her. 'We need to talk to this lady about what happened last night.'

The nurse was unhappy. 'We don't really allow more than three visitors at a time.' Nur Rashidah offered to leave.

'We'll need to talk to you as well,' Summers told her sharply. 'If you're Nur Rashidah Aziz, that is.' Her face became anxious at the tone.

'We're talking to all the witnesses,' said O'Connor, smiling at her reassuringly. 'But we can talk to you later, Miss Aziz, if you'll give us a contact number. Would this afternoon be a good time?'

They arranged a time, and Nur Rashidah gathered up her things preparatory to departing. 'I will leave a message for your mother at the hotel,' she told me.

'No, I need to phone her. To tell her not to come until tomorrow.'

She smiled, shaking her head. 'But she will want to come here *now*. She is your *mother*, she will not feel happy, knowing that you are here, ill; she will want to come.'

She didn't even know my mother, but of course she was right. I sighed, and Nur Rashidah smiled again. 'I will leave her a message.' She bent down and kissed me on the cheek, as naturally as a niece taking leave of a beloved aunt.

'Nur Rashidah,' I said as she reached the door, and she turned back to give me a look of enquiry.

'Don't marry any man who condescends to you,' I told her fiercely. 'You're worth much, *much* more than that.'

She smiled. 'Oh, Toni! Thank you.' She sailed out, still smiling.

'We need a statement from you about what happened last night,' Summers said brusquely, when she'd gone.

I told him a very simple version: I was sure he already had a detailed one. Thomas was wearing the same jeans and sweatshirt he'd had on the night before, and he'd arrived with the two detectives. I figured he'd probably spent the night at the police station.

'How did you know Mr Holden was in trouble?' Summers asked me, when I'd finished.

'Just a feeling.' I was not willing to tell this cold, sharp man about the murdered child. 'I thought that even if I was just being paranoid, it didn't cost me anything to go into the office and check.'

'And you told Miss Aziz to phone Emergency Services?'

'No. There wasn't time. Did she?'

'You didn't?' asked Thomas in surprise. 'You were telling that guy Howarth you had!'

'I was bluffing. Nur Rashidah phoned them?'

'Yeah. You just came straight in?'

'I didn't think there was time to do anything else.'

Thomas made a little *ha-huh* sound which wasn't laughter. 'He was just about to shoot me. That was what I thought, anyway. He says now that he wouldn't have.'

'He *was* going to shoot you,' I said, remembering the moment with a cold, sick lurch. If I'd been just a few seconds later, this sweet idealistic young man would have been coughing his life out on the floor. 'He'd asked about the disk, hadn't he?'

'Yeah. Soon as I came in and saw him. He put down the computer, pulled out the gun, and asked me about the disk.'

'If you'd told the police that, they would've known that it wasn't just an ordinary burglary. If you were found shot dead, they'd think it could have been.'

Thomas shivered. 'I *knew* you saved my life. I mean, I came in and he was taking the computer, and I . . . well, I'm sure you guessed that already. I keep seeing it.'

'How did he get in? The door was locked when we arrived; I *saw* you unlock it!'

'Back door. I don't suppose you even knew about the back door. All the buildings on the row have back doors on to this little alley where they keep the dustbins. He'd taken a crowbar or something to it; it's wrenched right out of the frame.'

Summers had been listening to this with an expression of cynicism and impatience. 'I agree with Ms Lanchester's view of the matter – but what *would have happened* is not going to be admissable in a court of law. All we can do is establish that Mr Howarth threatened you with the gun, until Ms Lanchester came in and told him that the police were on the way and that he would escape with a lighter penalty if he surrendered himself – correct, Ms Lanchester? Mr Holden told us you seemed to know all about the murder of Mr Norman.'

'I'd told you I suspected Howarth. Because of the questions he was asking. I gave you that piece of paper with his writing.'

'Which matches the writing on the note you received *exactly*,' put in O'Connor, with satisfaction. 'It was good enough that we got a search warrant on the strength of it.

Summers allowed himself a small, smug smile, and I understood that their search had found evidence linking Howarth with the murder.

'When did you get this search warrant?' I asked suspiciously.

'Saturday. Why?'

'I was wondering why Howarth decided to go looking for the mythical computer disk. If he knew he was being investigated, he must've decided that he *had* to get rid of whatever it was Ken had been using to blackmail him, before the police could find it.'

Summers gave me a look of level suspicion. 'Mr Holden said you also had some knowledge of what that was.'

'No. No knowledge. Just a guess – no, not even that! An intuition.'

I told them about my conversation with Elsie Norman, and about the pictures on Ken's computer. 'It just felt . . . *frightening*. I don't know why. Maybe because there were no human figures in the pictures, or almost none. And Ken *didn't* go mountain climbing when I knew him. I don't think he even could have: he wasn't fit enough. Something must have made him give it up. When Mrs Norman told me he'd gone mountain climbing with Howarth when they were students, and that Howarth had got him his job . . . it just seemed to fit.'

'So what does your *intuition* tell you happened on this mountain-climbing expedition?'

I shook my head, moving slowly and carefully because of the pain behind my eyes. 'I don't know. My guess would be rape – that they met another climber who was on her own, and they went further than they intended, and then killed her to keep it secret. That's nothing more than a guess, though.

Ken was a misogynist and a bully, so I can imagine it. But it could be something quite different.'

'It was something Howarth couldn't bear the thought of anyone finding out,' Summers said thoughtfully. 'It ate at him so much he kept looking for a computer disk that never even existed. He couldn't relax until he was *certain* that all the evidence was gone. I wish we'd been able to find Norman's computers.'

'You didn't?'

Summers grimaced, and O'Connor shook his head.

'So you think this blackmail was nothing to do with the rainforest?' asked Thomas, sounding almost disappointed.

'Oh, he'd collected dirt about the illegal logging as well,' Summers said. 'Obviously he had! He was a blackmailer: he wanted anything that would give him power over other people. He blackmailed Howarth into giving him a job he didn't merit, and then he used the job to dig for dirt. I'd be very surprised if Howarth was the only victim – another reason I wish we had his computers.'

'If we had them, we might be able to find his stash, too,' added O'Connor. 'Me, I'm sure he had one. Sure, he was more interested in power than money, but people like him, they want the money too.'

Summers was silent a moment, frowning, and then said abruptly, 'I'll get a list of the climbing expeditions Norman went on with Howarth.'

'Ah, John, it must've been thirty years ago!' objected O'Connor.

'If it was through a university society, there's probably a record. I'll see about it. Then we can see if there were any solo climbers who went missing at the same time.'

'Lot of work,' said O'Connor, mildly dismayed.

'I don't *like* the son of a bitch. What the intuitive lady said is right, too: he *will* get off with a couple of years for manslaughter, probably in an open prison, unless we get something else to nail him with. I'm going to work on it.'

The police left after that. Thomas remained. He sat down in the chair Nur Rashidah had occupied earlier and gazed at me earnestly.

'Last night I thought you were dying!' he told me.

'I *am* dying,' I reminded him gently. 'You've known that ever since we met.'

'I know, but I want you to live as long as you can. I wish . . . I wish that damned cancer would go into remission!'

I sighed. 'I wish, too, but . . . I made a mess of my life, you know. I can't even claim that I *deserve* some miraculous second chance.'

'Working for Masterpiece Home Design, you mean.'

'That was the last bad decision. There were others before that.' I hesitated, then confessed my sins. 'I wanted to write poetry: I settled for doing PR. I married a man because he was charming and attractive, and shut my eyes to his faults – then divorced him, bitterly and painfully, for the same faults I should have taken into account from the beginning. I've ignored my family for years, and abandoned friends. Oh, let me be honest: most of my life I've been looking for money and status instead of . . . of what *you've* been looking for: the good of something bigger than yourself; a chance to make a difference for the better.'

Thomas had listened to this in bewilderment. He sat back for a long moment, frowning hard. Then he asked, 'You know what the most valuable wood in the world is?'

I was surprised. 'No. Mahogany? Rosewood?'

'Eaglewood. It's also called agarwood and aloewood. It's an evergreen, grows on the lower slopes of the mountains in Southeast Asia. Now, normally, it's a perfectly ordinary tree – I mean, it's a nice tree, but nothing special. Not like a big dipterocarp or a camphor laurel. Sometimes, though, it gets infected with a fungus, and then it produces a resin to protect itself, and this stuff has a fragrance which is out of this world. They use it in perfumes, and ounce for ounce it's worth more than gold.'

'And my life is an eaglewood?'

'Well, I, uh, thought it might make you feel better to look at it like that.'

I considered it. The astrocytoma had infected me, and what I'd produced in response was worth more than gold. I thought of the stack of cards, the newspaper reports on 'how to make sure *your* furniture is green'. Yes. That *was* worth more than what I'd had alone in my lovely flat.

Perhaps it did make me feel better.

'This tree is endangered, of course?'

Thomas grinned and shrugged. 'Yeah. Of course. Well, you know, people in those countries are very poor. And you can't tell if a tree's infected just by looking at it, so of course you have to chop it down to see. There's a project to try to grow it in plantations, though: one of our partners is involved in that.'

'Good for them. Look, Thomas, I'll probably get some more cards like the ones I gave you last night, and I'm going to appeal for donations to the Rainforest Trust if I do any more interviews. I'm going to ask for donations instead of flowers at the funeral, too. We're going to have to get you some kind of legal standing to take the money. Can you ask Rafi how we could arrange that?'

'Sure. But . . .'

He hated any reference to my impending death. I didn't want to have to try to reassure him about it, so I said firmly, 'Right now I think you should go home and get some rest. You were up all night, weren't you? And Irene is probably worried.'

'Oh, I phoned her!' he reassured me. 'I am tired, though.' He looked at me uncertainly. 'You'll be all right?'

'I'm fine. My mother will be along this afternoon. And you have my contact numbers and address. Don't worry: I'll stay in touch.'

When he had gone, I looked over at the wall of the hospital room, where the rainforest was still waiting for me. The little boy was sitting on one of the great tree roots, weaving a necklace of flowers. He felt my eyes on him and looked up, smiling.

'Soon,' I told him. 'I need to spend a bit of time with my mother first.'

He nodded, and then he and the trees faded slowly, leaving only the blank white wall.

Soon, I repeated to myself. I would set the rest of my affairs in order, and then I would let the child take my hand.

I was not angry or afraid any more. I was even looking forward to it – to stepping out into that green dusk, to finally smelling the scent of resin and camphor, and feeling the softness of the ground under my feet, the warm moist air against my skin. The boy's small fingers would curl confidently about my own, and he would show me the way home.

Perhaps I was wrong to imagine that. Perhaps there would be nothing but the night. But to sleep, too, is good.